DITCH RIDER

A Ten Year Old Pioneer Boy's Quest to Manhood

By Steven R. Stewart

The YA Story for the Entire Family to Read Together

Ditch Rider

TABLE OF CONTENT

Prologue iv

Acknowledgment v

Chapter 1   Sunday 6

Chapter 2   Monday 19

Chapter 3   Tuesday 26

Chapter 4   Wednesday 33

Chapter 5   Thursday Morning 39

Chapter 6   Thursday Afternoon 52

Chapter 7   Friday Morning 65

Chapter 8   Friday Noon 73

Chapter 9   Friday Afternoon 84

Chapter 10   Friday Night 98

Chapter 11   Saturday Morning 102

Chapter 12   Saturday Afternoon 109

Chapter 13   After Quarantine 121

Epilogue 126

Bibliography 127

Prologue

Ditch Ride is a young adult historical fiction based on written family narratives and family lore supported by in-depth historical and geographical research.

All **Ditch Rider** characters are real, except for Abraham Washington, the black man traveling with the carnival. However, there was a black man carnival worker that caused a stir of curiosity with the town's people, but there is no written record of his name and actual encounter.

Tip was the name of the family dog, but horses' names: Lady, Dixie, and Casper were made up.

Most of the interactions and events are true, but several are embellished or fiction.

Acknowledgment

Ditch Rider front cover painting artist:

Vilonia Wilson

CHAPTER 1   SUNDAY

Jennie was only three years old – why did she have to die? Is *'life can be unfair'* the only answer?

The night Jennie turned for the worst, Dad's Model-T pickup truck wouldn't start, so Dad saddled Dixie and rode away to fetch Doctor Aikens. Twenty minutes later, the doctor's own Tin Lizzie chugged up in front of our house. The car doors clanged, and from my bedroom in our basement, I heard the clatter of shoes on the floor above as Dad and the doctor ran to the bedroom where Jennie laid.

Shuffling footsteps and a muffled conversation followed for a few minutes. And then all was quiet. I slipped from my warm heavy quilt. The stair treads were cold on my bare feet. I stepped onto the main level of our house and found Mama and Dad holding each other and crying at the front door. Doctor Aikens rested a hand on Dad's shoulder and spoke softly.

Jennie Spendlove, my three-year-old little sister, died Sunday, November 6, 1926. Jennie was sick for more than a week. Her throat was sore and swollen, and she'd complained her eyes and ears hurt badly. Mama and Dad and Doctor Aikens thought she would get better, but she didn't. I was ten years old, and that night, for the first time in my life, I saw my Dad cry. It scared me—

and at the top of the stairs, I burst into tears and cried hard.

Mom turned toward me. "Come here, Earl," she said and opened an arm to me. I ran across the living room, and she pulled me to her side.

Doctor Aikens unbuckled his large black leather bag and pulled out a yellow sheet of paper and said to Dad, "I'm sorry George, but no one can leave this house for the next seven days. I need you to post this on your front door. Marshall Scow should have posted it last week." The yellow piece of paper said the house was under something called "quarantine."

Dad squints his eyes and reads, PUBLIC NOTICE, written across the top of the page. The paper jittered in his thick, callused hands. He lifted his gaze to Doctor Aikens. "We can't stay in the house for the entire week, Doc. The animals have to be looked after, and weeds have sprung up in the sugar beet field from the last little bit of rain." Tears escaped Dad's eyes and streaked down his face. He took Mama's hand and said, "And we have to have a funeral for our little lamb."

"George," Doctor Aikens said, "diphtheria is highly contagious, and think how you would feel if someone in your family passed it to someone else's little girl or boy. I'll come back later this morning and examine everyone in the family." He held up a hand when Dad tried to say something. "I know no one else appears infected; we just can't be too sure. Diphtheria is spread by airborne germs so you can go outside on your property, but you have to keep your distance from other people. And more importantly, no one can enter this house for the next seven days."

I had only seen my mother cry what she called tears of joy. Mama and Dad both cried hard. I hugged Mama's waist and cried with them. Mama whimpered, "Shush. We need to be careful not to wake your sisters."

My eight-year-old sister Shirley and five-year-old sister Ruth were asleep in their bed also in the basement. The basement stayed cool year-round, and we stored butter and cheese and canned goods there. When Jennie got sick, Mama made a bedroom for Shirley and Ruth in our basement storage room.

Dad was a strong, hardworking farmer, carpenter, and mason. He built our house and several families and neighbors' houses in our little town of Hurricane, Utah. Dad usually stood straight and confident, but that night he stooped and looked tired.

I didn't know what to say to help Dad feel better, so I just said, "I'm sorry, Dad." My eyes tightened and wanted to cry again, but I wouldn't let them. "It'll be alright," I told him.

Dad looked down at me. His eyebrows were thick and his face golden from years of work in the desert sun. "I'll be fine, son—don't worry about me. It's going to be hard for all the family." He fought back tears as a soft smile spread across his face, not one with his lips which showed his teeth, but a heartwarming smile with his cheeks and gaze of his light blue eyes which told me, *I'm proud of you*. I couldn't help myself, and I cried hard. Dad's thick, solid hand squeezed my shoulder. We all cried.

Mama tugged me against her again. I gazed up at Mama's large brown eyes, which always made me feel safe. Her eyes and face were sad and wet. She was a pretty woman. She was thirty-seven years old, but her hair turned gray ten years earlier—just after I was born. Mama suffered from malaria, and the high fever stripped the color from her hair.

She leaned down and whispered, "Sweetie, it's late, you need to run back to bed and go to sleep," and kissed my cheek.

I hugged her and said, "Good night." I walked to the stairs to the basement; at the top, I turned and watched Mama. She held Dad's hand and walked with her slight limp into Jennie's room. In her late teens, Mama contracted a mild case of polio. She had grown to her full height, so her legs were the same length, but the muscles in her right leg were smaller than those in her left. I never once heard her complain, though. Always positive, she said she was just thankful at least her legs were the same length.

I stepped down the first two steps and paused. Peeking

through the spindles, I watched Mama and Dad in Jennie's room. Dad lifted a small tin can from the bedside table. A few coins rattled inside. Mama and Dad had bribed Jennie—first with pennies, then with nickels—to take her medicine, bitter medicine that made her scrunch her face and shiver. Dad bent down and picked up Jennie's small, brown, hand-me-down shoes and gazed at the scuffed toes. Mama took a pair of scissors from the bedside table and cut a lock of Jennie's hair and tied a pink ribbon around it. With Jennie's small white hairbrush, Mama tenderly brushed Jennie's hair and sobbed.

I returned downstairs and crawled into my bed and cried myself to sleep.

It felt like no time before Shirley and Ruth woke me from a hard sleep. They were both upstairs crying real loud. It wasn't unusual for Shirley to whine or cry, but not Ruth. And then, my one-year-old baby sister, LaDean, began crying too.

The sweet smoke of side meat Mama frying on the wood stove helped me get out of bed. I pulled on my shirt and pants and plodded up the cool stair treads.

LaDean usually woke early, and Mama would have fed her and changed her diaper before I woke up. I asked Mama if she thought LaDean might be crying because somehow she knew Jennie died. Mama said, "No, Honey, she heard your sisters, and sometimes babies cry when they're tired."

I told Mama, "I'm too tired to cry when I'm tired."

* * *

A knock on our front door reminded me every Sunday morning, my second cousin, Willie Isom, came to our house and walked to church with me. His parents made him go to church, and he knew we'd be going—so he always walked with me.

I raced to the front door. "I'll get it."

Mama yelled from the kitchen, "Don't you open the door."

With my hand on the doorknob, I said to Mama, "I need to tell Willie I can't walk to church with him."

"You tell him from the front window."

"Okay, I will."

Peering out the window, I saw Willie scrubbed clean with dripping wet hair combed straight back. He wore his white Sunday shirt and brown necktie. I tugged open the window and stuck my head out. My eyes swelled with tears, and my voice caught as it trembled. "Hey, Willie, we can't go to church today. Jennie died."

Willie's eyebrows tightened. "Jennie died? Ooh, I'm sorry. I knew she was really sick."

"Doctor Aikens made us put the yellow piece of paper you see on our front door. It says we can't breathe around other people for seven days. "

Willie's shoulders slumped. "I wanted to show you something real swell after church."

"What?"

My mother called from the kitchen, "Earl, get out of that window and tell Willie he needs to go to church without you."

"Okay, Mama." And then I spoke low to Willie. "What is it?"

"A traveling carnival has set up at town square, and they have a black man working for them!"

"A real black man?" I said.

"Yeah," Willie said. He glanced around and whispered. "He's real black and real strong." Willie balled his fist and cocked his arms like a strongman in a sideshow.

It was unusual for a carnival to come to our tiny desert town, and to have a black person was something special. Less than a thousand people lived in Hurricane—pronounced, *hurr-i-kun*, the British pronunciation, not *hurr-i-cane*. Many of the area's settlers, like my grandfathers and grandmothers Spendlove and Isom, were from England and Wales, and the town name long since stuck.

Wide-eyed, Willie said, "He's the first black person I've ever seen in real life. Have you ever seen one before?"

"No . . ." I whispered.

"Earl, go get me a switch from the mulberry tree," Mama said. "I told you to get out of the window."

"Okay, okay, I'm done now, Mama," I said over my shoulder, and looked at Willie. "I gotta go—maybe he'll be there next week." I pulled the window, sash down.

Through the window glass, I saw Willie shake his head and mouth the word, *no*.

* * *

Our family sat quietly at the kitchen table and ate lunch. Dad told Mama, "I can't stay on our property this Friday. I promised Will Hinton I would ride the canal for him."

The canal was dug into the walls of the Virgin River Canyon to bring drinking water to Hurricane and to irrigate the fields and fruit trees. Someone had to ride the canal on horseback every day and look for leaks and rock slides. Will Hinton worked for the Hurricane Canal Company, and sometimes Dad or Grandpa rode it for him if he needed to take care of personal business.

Ever since I was a little boy, I'd wanted to ride with Dad and check on the canal, and by golly, I snapped to attention when Dad said, "Maybe it's time to let Earl ride with me. Grandpa said he wants to ride with me for old times' sake, and he has already been exposed to Jennie, so that won't matter." Dad choked up. "We'll avoid anyone we meet when we ride the couple blocks to Hurricane Hill."

Mama's face gave no sign of approval. My fingertips fluttered on the tabletop, and my legs trembled.

I was the shortest boy in the fourth grade, but I knew I was big enough to go—besides, I could ride a horse as well as the next fellow. I hated my darn, short legs. But I could run as fast as any boy in my class.

"We have five days," Mama said, "so let's talk about it later."

"I'm big enough; please let me go," popped from my mouth.

"We'll think about it, and don't ask me again."

Mama cleared the table and avoided eye contact with Dad or me.

Mama always stayed busy taking care of the family. The only time she sat down was to eat meals, to sew things, or to read her Sunday school lessons. She expected us to go to church every Sunday; that Sunday, we had to stay at home.

Mama and Dad had to feel my stare as they moved about the house. I was dying to ride the seven and one-half miles through the steep canyon with Dad and Grandpa.

I gazed out the dining room window at Hurricane Hill, which was a little more than a half-mile from our house. I didn't know why they called it a hill—it was as high as a lot of mountains. The canal sliced a gently sloping line across the hill's dry, rugged face and turned and disappeared into the Virgin Narrows. Local pioneers and old-timers called Hurricane Canal the *ditch*, so riding the *ditch* was the same thing as riding to inspect the canal.

The muddy Virgin River flows from Zion Canyon National Park ten miles upstream, enters the flat desert, and cuts its way through the sandy desert soil. The river's sandy banks are low and loose. Early pioneers settled along the river and lost their farms and homes from sudden hard rain and floods.

It took eleven years to build the three and one-half miles of canal through the canyon, and another four-mile stretch across the base of Hurricane Hill. And when that was completed, they dug irrigation trenches across the flat desert future town of Hurricane.

Grandpa Spendlove had once said that twenty-two years ago, when the canal's precious water first spilled through Hurricane's irrigation trenches, there wasn't a single tree. And now every yard had at least one nice, tall shade tree, and there were orchards, vineyards, and fields of alfalfa and field crops.

Grandma Spendlove loved to laugh and say, "Under the shade of a barbwire fence was all we had to visit with neighbors." She also liked to say, "If the canal's water ever stops flowing, our little town of Hurricane will dry up and blow away."

That's why the canal was so important to us.

Seventy-four years ago, the leaders of our Mormon Church in Salt Lake City asked for volunteers to move to southern Utah to try and grow cotton. They named the area the Cotton Mission, but soon everyone called the area Dixie. The cotton didn't do too well, but like the old southern states, Dixie, a lot of peaches were grown.

* * *

I had no idea what a test of my nerves a week quarantined with sourpuss Shirley, and even sweet Ruth would be. Despite my daily chores and the extra things Dad found for me to do, there was way too much sister exposure. Everyone was so sad around the house, and I thought I would go nuts if I didn't get to escape with Dad to ride the canal Friday.

Fortunately, the week before our quarantine, a large box of used library books arrived at our house. Mama loved books, and she always read to us before bedtime, which taught us kids, to love to read. She found a magazine advertisement offering free used books from the Salt Lake County Library. Mama mailed a list of her children's names and ages and two dollars for postage and handling. Three weeks later, here came this big box wrapped in heavy brown paper, addressed: The Spendlove Family.

It was like Christmas. Mama snipped the cord wrapped around our special package and told us Ruth had been the sweetest lately so she could rip off the wrapping paper. Shirley and I knelt close to the brown box. And like under the tree, Christmas morning, Mama passed out each book to whom it best belonged.

There were books and magazines for everyone in the family,

including several issues of *Boy's Life* magazine. I read and reread every one of them cover-to-cover. At the bottom of the box, I found a copy of Victor Hugo's *Les Miserables.* I decided someday I would have to read it to see why Lester was so miserable.

The 1925 issues of *Boy's Life* celebrated the fifteenth anniversary of the founding of the Boy Scouts of America. One issue was full of nifty facts about the huge country of China. The article said the rest of the world knew little of the people living there and called China the "lonesome corner of the world." But it turned out a population explosion was happening in that poorest of countries, and the Boy Scouts was growing fast there.

I wondered what Mama and Dad had heard of the place, so when Dad came in the house through the back door for a late lunch, I said, "Hey Dad, have you ever heard much about China?"

"Earl, I'm sorry, but I'm not interested in China right now. Share it with Shirley and Ruth. We can talk about China another time."

"Okay," I said. And judging by his tone, I figured it wasn't time to ask if I could ride the canal with Dad on Friday.

I carried the magazine to the playpen, where LaDean laid asleep on her back, and I glanced at Shirley and Ruth playing with their dolls on the floor. With my forearms resting on the crib's top rail, and my China article held in both hands, I glanced down at LaDean, then to my *Boy's Life,* and then back to LaDean. "Uh-huh," I said loudly each time I looked down at LaDean. My sisters looked at me. Once I knew I had their attention, I nodded and said, "Yep, it's true."

"What?" Shirley said. Ruth sat up to listen.

"Have you ever noticed how big LaDean's dark brown eyes are? Now it makes sense," I said and stared at my China article.

Shirley and Ruth climbed to their knees and peered between the slats at LaDean.

"Yeah," Shirley said, "Dad says she has the biggest brown eyes he's ever seen on a little girl."

"You know why, don't you?"

"Why?" Ruth said, her crystal blue eyes excited.

"Because she's a Chinaman."

"Nuh-uh," Shirley and Ruth said in unison.

"It's true. You don't have to believe me? It says here that every fifth child born in the world today is a Chinaman—think about it. LaDean was the fifth child born in our family. Yep, that makes her a Chinaman. Sure does explain her big brown eyes and dark hair."

"Oh, no," Ruth said.

Shirley pressed her cheeks against the slats and looked puzzled.

I shook my head. "I just hope we can teach her to speak English."

* * *

When Mama tucked me into bed and helped me say my prayers, Dad stood at my doorway and listened sad looking. He didn't always help say our prayers; he did that night and held his hands clasped.

I saw Mama take a breath, pause, and tremble as she said, "Earl, we need to remember to pray for Jennie. She's now playing with the other children in heaven."

I folded my arms and closed my eyes tight and prayed. "God bless me to grow up to be a good man." I felt Mama shaking and softly sobbing. I asked God to, "Bless Jennie in heaven and bless Mama and Dad to be happy again. Bless Shirley, Ruth, LaDean, and Grandma Petty, and Grandma and Grandpa Spendlove, my cousins, the crops in the fields and all our animals, and everything good, in the name of Jesus Christ, amen."

"Goodnight, Earl," Dad said faintly as he left my doorway.

After Mama kissed me goodnight and went to help my sisters with their prayers, I got busy and prayed again, asking God to let me ride the canal with Dad and Grandpa Friday. And then I cried again.

That night Mama and Dad let Shirley and Ruth sleep in their bed. Mama and Dad sat on our kitchen chairs in the front room with Jennie's body, praying for her. Several times I heard them crying—they called it a vigil.

* * *

After I finished half of my morning barnyard chores, I slipped into the house for another biscuit. Mama, Shirley, and Ruth were busy with the wash. Monday was always wash day, and Mama said it was a good time for the girls to talk and be together. Shirley and Ruth said they didn't feel like doing the wash; they were still too sad. But Mama insisted and said everyone needed to stay busy to keep their mind off things.

With buckets of hot water from our cast iron wood stove, Mama filled our large No. 3 washtub placed on the kitchen table. She made the water soapy by scrubbing a large bar of homemade soap against the ribs of a scrub board stood in the hot water. Her hands turned bright pink.

While I spread jam on the leftover biscuit, I heard Mama say, "You girls separate the white clothes from the dark ones. Make me two piles right here." Shirley took my other pair of everyday pants from the dirty clothes basket, and Mama said, "Search Earl's pants pockets for rocks. I'm sure he hasn't emptied them as I tell him to do every day."

"Why should I have to search his old dumb pockets?" Shirley said. "He's always looking for rocks and arrowheads, rocks and arrowheads. What's so pretty about a dumb rock?"

"Oh, it's not going to kill you."

"Ooo," Shirley said. "There's dirt and rocks in his pockets."

I didn't say anything as I walked to the back door. Ruth picked up little Jennie's play dress and held it in front of her. Ruth's face crumbled, and she and Shirley both began to cry.

Mama wrapped the girls in her arms and kissed the tops of their heads. She sobbed with the girls, and said, "It's okay, it's okay. Let's put it aside, and I'll wash it later."

I felt tears building, so I stepped outside, but before I was down the steps, I burst into tears, too.

Many times I helped Mama with the wash. She always asked for the white things first. She would drop the pieces in the washtub and churned them in hot water, squeezing and twisting each piece. She would examine each one, and if she didn't think a piece of clothing was clean enough, it would scrubbed up and down the scrub board's metal ribs. Scrubbing the clothes made the sound of a fluttering bumblebee, and the metal ribs tended to wear out the cloths. Mom only did it when needed. The clean pieces were placed in the kitchen sink full of fresh cool water, rinsed, twisted tight, and dropped into a large straw basket. Laundry day was hard work.

An hour later, as I raked out the barn, I saw Mama and the girls walk to the metal wire clothesline strung between two trees. Mama sang her favorite hymns as the girls pinned the clothes to the heavy wire. When done, with a forked limp post, she hoisted the clothes six or seven feet above the ground to dry in the desert breeze. After the clothes dried, a half-day was required to iron them.

Once done with my chores, I stepped into the kitchen, and Mama greeted me with, "Here's my little fibber, now."

"What do you mean?" I said.

"Liar, liar, pants on fire," Shirley said and made one of her less-pleasant faces—one that showed you if there was a booger up her nose.

It was quite for a moment as the three of them stared at me. "Why did you tell your little sisters LaDean is a Chinaman?"

I flared my eyes, trying to look surprised she asked. "I just told them what I read in *Boy's Life*. It said every fifth person born in the world is a Chinaman, and LaDean was the fifth person born in our family." I made a puzzled face. "They wouldn't print it if it wasn't true."

Mama shook her head and fought a smile. "You stop being so silly and worrying these girls."

Shirley chimed in, "Dad always says, if you aren't honest, you aren't anything!"

"I just told you what the magazine said."

"Go, go on." Mama flipped her hands at me. "You're supposed to be the big brother and look after your sisters." She paused, and we both realized I couldn't look after all my sisters, now Jennie left us. I shrugged my shoulders. I couldn't say anything. I turned and headed for the spot on the floor beneath the living room window, where I stacked my books and magazines.

Mama said, "And you find somewhere to keep your books, not in my living room."

CHAPTER 2   MONDAY

The delicious aroma from upstairs told me it was time to get dressed for my morning chores. Before yesterday, I would have heard Jennie's soft little bare feet pattering around the kitchen as I lay under my warm covers. When I thought of not ever hearing or seeing Jennie again, it made me feel sad—tired and weak. I cried a little before I got out of bed.

Monday, a steady stream of well-wishers in our front yard kept Mama and Dad at our front door, visiting with family and friends from church. Many of the folks left food, flowers, and sympathy cards at the bottom of our front porch steps. Marion and Mary Stout, our neighbors across the street with fifteen children of their own, were the first to visit and asked to help any way they could. They returned every day that week.

Mama and Dad tried to be strong, but they wept most times someone came by to pay their respects.

From the living room window, Dad saw Uncle Charles, one of Mama's brothers, close the front gate behind him and stroll toward our front door. He wore his usual baggy brown suit with a vest, necktie, and fedora. Uncle Charles was a successful businessman. He owned the town's movie theater, a drugstore, the Hurricane Ford Motors, and Dodge dealership, and Arrow Gas and Oil with partner Stanley Bradshaw.

"Here comes Old Money Bags," Dad muttered. He called to the back of the house. "Lilly, your brother Charles is out front."

With her usual limp, Mama shuffled from the kitchen, wiping her hands with her apron. "I'm coming."

Hearing Dad's announcement, we kids raced to the door. Dad was never too excited, but we always loved Uncle Charles's visits.

"You children don't need to come to the door," Mama said.

"But Mama," I cried.

"This is not the time—"

Dad opened the door. "Hello, Charles. Please don't come any closer than the bottom of the steps. Doctor Aikens' orders—we're quarantined."

"I have heard," Uncle Charles said. He removed his hat and held it down at his side. "Hello, Lilly. I'm so sorry to hear about sweet little Jennie. I hope the other children are well and healthy."

"We're fine, Charles," Mama said.

"Hey, Uncle Charles," I called out, peeking around Dad.

"Hello, kids," he said.

Uncle Charles wasn't a tall man. He always walked with his hands shoved into his suit coat pockets. Dad said he did so he could squeeze the first penny he ever made.

"Where's Maggie?" Mama asked.

"I came straight from work, so she is at home. She sends her love and sympathy to both of you. She'll be here for the funeral service tomorrow." Uncle Charles' face wasn't bright like it usually was—his eyes lids looked heavy, and his mouth was turned down. "What time is the service?"

"Ten in the morning," Dad said.

Uncle Charles nodded and gazed up from the walkway. I think I saw his eyes tear up.

"But, the other children are well?" He said.

"None of the symptoms we saw with Jennie," Mama said.

"Doctor Aikens will examine us again Wednesday morning."

Uncle Charles nodded and looked lost for words. "All the family is praying for you."

"We feel their love with us. We're blessed with wonderful friends and family," Mama said.

"We truly are," Uncle Charles said. "Is there anything I can do for you, or go get for you? You need anything from the store?"

Mama glanced at Dad for any suggestions. Dad shook his head.

"No, we are in good order here," Mama said. "My kitchen table is covered with food everyone has brought for us, but thank you, Charles."

Shirley popped out to the side of Mama. "Do we get to play scramble?"

A smile spread across Uncle Charles' face. He pressed his hat onto his head, shoved his hands into his pockets, and jingled coins.

"This is not the time for that," Mama said and straightened her shoulders.

"Oh, sure it is, Lilly," he said. "The kids need to have fun—this has been difficult for them, too."

"Please, Mama," Ruth said.

"Well, okay." Mama waved off Uncle Charles. She stepped to the side and let us kids escape onto the porch. "Charles, you back up a few steps. Be careful, and no one gets hurt."

Uncle Charles slipped his hand around inside his right suit coat pocket. He drew out a dinner roll and dropped it into his left pocket. Whenever Uncle Charles ate at a restaurant, he would slip any leftover dinner rolls into his pocket.

Dad snickered and whispered to Mama, "He's your brother, not mine."

Uncle Charles reached into his right pants pocket shook and fumbled coins and after some time of jiggling and separating coins drew out his clenched fist. "Are you ready, kids?"

"Yes!" we yelled. "Ready!"

He grinned and counted, "One, two, three." He took one step forward and showered the front porch with nickels, dimes, and pennies. "Scramble!" he said.

We dropped to our knees and scrambled to scoop up the coins. I ended up with three dimes and a nickel, Shirley had two nickels, three pennies, and one dime. But Ruth only had two pennies and one nickel, so I gave her one of my dimes.

Uncle Charles threw a hand in the air, waved goodbye, and walked toward his car. "Take care," he chuckled to us over his shoulder.

"What do you say, children?" Mama said.

"Thank you, Uncle Charles!"

Mama and Dad herded us inside the house.

"Never quarters or half dollars," Dad said and chuckled. "Earl, check your nickel and see if Uncle Charles has squeezed it so hard it popped out your buffalo's eyeball."

"George," Mama said.

It was Dad's first light-hearted moment since Jennie died.

I plopped down on the floor with the living room window to my back for better reading light. I dug through my pile of books and magazines. Shirley and Ruth ran to their room. I heard their coins chink in their piggy banks one at a time.

Dad eased onto our upholstered chair in the living room. His little bit of a smile faded. He spoke before Mama reached the kitchen. "I was surprised Charles made a special trip to visit us. He works night and day, and we'll see him tomorrow."

"That was nice of him," Mama said. "Wouldn't you imagine Jennie's passing is a little more difficult for him than most of our family?"

Dad looked at Mama in thought. He nodded slowly. "I haven't thought of that. Losing Jennie must have stirred difficult memories for him."

Mama glanced at me as if she wondered had I heard their conversation. I stared at my magazine. Mama returned to her work in the kitchen. I wondered what was more difficult for Uncle Charles, but I didn't think I should ask.

* * *

At dusk, a small white wooden coffin was delivered to our front porch. The pretty little box looked sad and lonely there by itself. Dad opened the front door and stared. He stepped onto the porch. While tears streamed down his cheeks, he bent and picked up the coffin. He cradled it in his arms and gazed as if he held Jennie. After a few moments, he carried the coffin to Jennie's room and closed the door behind him.

* * *

At bedtime, I prayed again for Jennie in heaven and asked Heavenly Father to help make my mother and father happy. Mama tucked me in and kissed me good night.

I laid in the dark, unable to sleep. My bedroom doorknob clicked, and light from the hallway spread across my face. Dad stood in the doorway. The light behind him was bright, but his face was dim in his own shadow. Dad's kind voice said, "Earl, are you asleep?" He held the doorknob in one hand and leaned against the door frame in his faded overalls.

"No, sir," I said. "I can't get to sleep."

"Son, I want you to stop worrying about your mother and me," he said. "We'll be fine. We'll all be fine." Dad gazed a moment. "I tell you what, son; you go ahead and plan on riding the canal with me and Grandpa Spendlove on Friday afternoon."

My eyes popped wide open. "Really? Thank you, Dad!" I struggled to an elbow.

Dad set his back against the door frame, crouched a little, and scrubbed his back side-to-side as he often did to scratch an itch. He straightened and shrugged his shoulders and appeared relieved. "You'll need to bring your heavy coat and an extra blanket. Nights in the canyon get much colder than here in Hurricane."

I had heard the nights were cold in the Virgin River Canyon because sunlight reached the floor of the deep, narrow canyon for a short time each day.

"We won't be able to return home before dark, so we'll probably spend the night at Chinatown Wash campsite."

The old Mormon pioneers often sat around and talked about the early days and the eleven years it took to build the canal with dynamite, picks, and shovels. As the work progressed through the canyon, the workers nicknamed the campsites: Duffin's Flat, Robber's Roost, Chinatown Wash, LeVerkin Hot Springs, and Gould's Wash.

"Yes, sir, thank you. Yippee!"

"Now try not to think too much and get to sleep. You still have your morning chores."

"Yes, sir."

"Goodnight, son." Dad pulled the door closed behind him.

I shuffled my feet back and forth beneath my covers. *I'm going to ride the canal. I'm going to ride the canal! I can't wait to tell the boys at school, darn! I can't go to school this week and tell anyone. I better take my BB gun.* Dad and Grandpa Spendlove always wore their pistols in case of a snake or a mountain lion.

I wondered if Dad would let Tip come, too. Tip was a good snake-sniffing dog. When we played in the canal or the Virgin River, old Tip would yelp and dance if a snake showed up. Dad called Tip a sooner dog, and said, "He'd sooner do it in the house as doing it in the yard." But I knew Dad was trying to be funny.

Offering another prayer, I thanked God for letting me ride the canal Friday. But then I remembered Jennie, and I felt bad about being so happy. I asked God why she had to die. Why did Mama and Dad have to lose their little girl? Why didn't Jennie get to grow up and be a mama?

CHAPTER 3   TUESDAY

Jennie's funeral was Tuesday morning, but we couldn't have it at the church or the cemetery because Doctor Aiken's quarantine notice was still tacked on our front door.

Mama bathed and dressed Jennie in a pretty white dress Uncle Charles and Aunt Maggie bought for her. Dad propped the small coffin in the living room window so family and friends in our front yard could see Jennie during the funeral service. We stayed inside and sang and prayed with them.

It was a sad day, and so hard on Mama and Dad.

Mama and Dad kissed Jennie goodbye and latched the coffin's lid. Brother Stout from across the street, drove the little coffin to the Hurricane Cemetery for burial. We had to stay at home.

* * *

Aunt Josephine Spendlove, one of Hurricane's three schoolteachers, was in the front yard for the funeral, and before leaving, she spoke to Mama and placed our school assignments on our steps. After everybody was gone, Mama sent me outside to bring in Aunt Josephine's large manila envelope. I followed Mama into the kitchen. Mama unwound the red string, opened the flap, and pulled out three sheets of lined school tablet paper. Aunt Josephine had written three separate pages of school assignments, one for each of us kids.

Mama glanced over the pages. She laid the pages on the kitchen table. "We'll have to look at these later today. I feel I may need to take a nap." Her eyes moistened, and she hurried to her bedroom and closed the door behind her.

I picked up my assignment sheet and read it. *Nothing unexpected there.* I picked up the envelope and went to place the assignment sheets inside, but its weight made me realize something else was inside.

I reached in and pulled out two report cards—our first ones for the year. Mine was on top. *Hmm, two A's and two B's. Comments: A good student, but his humor distracts others at times. Hmm.*

I opened Shirley's report card. "Horsefeathers!" *Three A's and one B. Comments: An excellent student. Comes prepared.*

Searching deeper in the large envelope, I found Ruth's report card, her first-ever. *All A's. Comments: A joy to have in class, helpful to others.* I figured as much.

"Hey girls," I hollered to the living room. "Your report cards are here."

Shirley and Ruth ran into the kitchen.

"Shirley, your teacher, Mrs. Hinton, says you'll have to retake all your tests."

"No, she did not," Shirley said and snatched her report card from me.

I opened little Ruth's card and acted as if I was reading it. I shook my head and said, "You can't be a member of our family with those grades—you'll have to find someplace else to live."

Ruth's brow scrunched, and her lips pursed. Her voice squeaked. "Really? What did I do wrong? I made good grades on my tests."

Mama must have heard us from her room and came to Ruth's rescue.

"Give me that," she said and plucked the card from my hand. She opened it and glanced at the grades. "Ruth, this is excellent—all A's. The best anybody can do. Sweetie, don't ever believe anything, Earl tells you like that. I ought to take a switch to his backside."

* * *

Mid-afternoon, Mama reviewed our week's school assignments with us. I was a decent student; arithmetic came easy to me, and I loved to read—not like a lot of my school chums. Shirley and Ruth actually loved schoolwork. Girls!

Without the distractions of our classmates, we zipped through our first lessons and left plenty of time to go outside and play in the backyard.

Shirley was always dependable to whine and complain—a real fuddy-duddy. It was hard for me to put up with a grumpy sister who was two years younger than me and two inches taller. Sweet Ruth was always the peacemaker, so she wasn't nearly as much fun to badger, plus she was short for her age, too.

When I complained to Mama and asked why was I so short, she suggested maybe if I hung by my hands from a tree limb or our swing set, I could stretch my bones and grow taller.

The mulberry tree outside our back door was popular with us kids, even if it was an endless supply of switches. We spent hours climbing that old tree or swinging from a rope tied to a limb. That afternoon I took Mama's old washtub—kept in the backyard to cook down lard and lye to make our soap—and turned it upside down at the base of the tree so I could climb up.

The tall-drink-of-water Shirley came out the back door and caught me hanging by my hands from the lowest limb of the mulberry tree, hoping to stretch a little taller. I didn't hear her walk up behind me as I hung there listening to the carnival music, the chatter of the crowd, and the ding of the bells on the midway two blocks away on the town square.

Shirley never passed up an opportunity to share her two cents' worth of opinion. "You don't believe hanging like that will make you taller, do you?"

Holy cow! I swung over and dropped down on the washtub. I spun around and said, "If it is any business of yours, I was doing pull-ups to build my muscles."

Shirley scrunched her face and shrugged her shoulders. I could tell she didn't believe me.

Ruth came out to play, so I went inside the house to find something else to entertain me, but it didn't take long before I became bored. I didn't feel like reading, and if I asked Mama for something to do, she would give me something no fun to do. Mom was in the front room, mending socks, so I stayed clear of there. I drank water at the kitchen sink, and, through the kitchen window, I saw Shirley sitting on the same limb she had caused me to give up, swinging her dangling feet and singing.

I had a great idea! I trotted downstairs and crawled beneath my bed and retrieved my Daisy Red Ryder BB gun, and ran upstairs.

I hadn't had money to buy BBs since summer, so there wasn't a chance of me shooting Shirley, but of course, she didn't know. I pushed open the screen door and stepped onto the porch.

"Look, Ruth!" I said. "There's a scrawny chicken in our tree."

I pressed the stock to my shoulder.

Shirley squawked like a hen laying a brick and held one hand in front of her.

I cocked my trusty Red Ryder.

Shirley squawked another octave higher.

"Stop it, Earl. Stop it," Ruth said.

"We'll have us long-legged, skinny chicken for supper," I said and laid a bead on Shirley. I closed one eye and squeezed the trigger.

Poof.

Nothing but a puff of air came out, but Shirley screeched and flailed her arms as she fell four feet and made a solid thud on the ground like a drunken rodeo clown.

"Good shot," I said.

Shirley struggled to her hands and knees. I think for a couple of seconds, her eyes crossed. She sputtered and spat dirt.

I knew I shouldn't have pointed my gun, loaded or unloaded, at Miss Smarty-pants, but I had to admit her sprawling flight was a thing of beauty.

Mama suddenly appeared behind the back door. "What in tarnation is going on out here?" She sized up the situation and slapped open the screen door. "Give me that," she said and snatched the rifle from my hands. "Did you shoot your sister?"

"I was teasing her! I don't have any BBs and only air came out."

With my gun in one hand, Mama popped me on my fanny with the other. "What do you use your brain for?" she said.

Ruth comforted Shirley and helped her to the back door.

Mama said, "Girls, come on; you deserve bread and jam." She glared at me. "You sit here on the porch, and don't you move a muscle until you explain to your father what you did today."

* * *

In the afternoon, Dad came home from chopping the weeds in the sugar beet field. Pink wrinkles around his eyes told me he had been crying.

Dad never spanked me with his hand, but I figured he would be sending me to pick my own mulberry switch. One of those snapped across your backside would get your attention while you danced a jig on your tippy-toes.

Before I could speak to Dad, Mama stepped out the back door. "George," she said. "Your son, Earl, shot Shirley with his BB gun, and she fell from the mulberry tree."

"But I didn't have any BBs!" I protested.

"Shirley didn't know," Mama said. "And she fell to the ground."

Dad's eyes appeared tired and weak. He looked disappointed and shook his head, and in a faint voice, he said to Mama, "Was Shirley hurt?"

"No, but she could have been."

"I'm sorry but . . . I'm not up to this now. Do what you think best, Lilly."

Mama saw Dad's pain and knew to let the matter drop. He lumbered down the steps to the basement.

Mama called to Dad, "Let's rethink if we should let Earl ride the canal Friday."

"Okay . . ." Dad said.

I didn't know what Mama would do. Her eyes welled with tears, and she rolled her hands tight in her apron. Her voice trembled as she said, "You girls set the table for supper, please. Earl, you go see if Tip has water in his bowl, and you'll clear the table and wash the dishes by yourself tonight."

When Mama called Dad for supper, he said from the basement to eat without him.

Little was said while we ate supper without Dad.

We heard Dad cranking the milk separator downstairs while he cried and talked loud and angry at God.

* * *

In the evening, us kids, even Shirley, stayed quiet and read our mail order books and magazines.

Dad went to his bedroom and closed the door. Mama fell asleep in our upholstered chair while reading her scriptures, so we kids put ourselves to bed.

After I said my prayers, I lay in bed and tried to hatch a plan to regain Mama and Dad's permission to ride the canal. How could I get back into their good grace?

Two possibilities came to mind: beg for forgiveness and deliver

Shirley a well-rehearsed "sincere" apology, or look pitiful and broken-hearted, mope around, and not speak to anyone. If I succeeded in getting to ride the canal, I figured my skinny-chicken-hunting expedition guaranteed my BB gun wouldn't be with me for the ride.

CHAPTER 4   WEDNESDAY

Wednesday afternoon, when it was our turn to receive irrigation water at our city lot, Dad walked one block up the street and opened the stop gate at the appointed time.

I waited for the ditch water, which ran along the edge of the street and our property. Soon the water arrived in a rushing hiss that covered the trench bottom and quickly swelled to a gurgling twelve-inch depth—a small river of precious water.

Twigs and leaves sailed downstream like tiny ships. At the ready, I launched an enemy ship I made of three sticks lashed together with dried grass. I opened fire with my arsenal of rocks stashed in my pockets.

"Boom . . . boom!" I said with each blast.

An unexpected thud splashed next to my enemy target. I looked upstream and found Willie Isom with a Cheshire cat's grin, and taking a second aim at my escaping foe.

I laughed. "What are you doing here?"

"I was on my way home from school and saw you waiting on the water."

Willie fired again. "Boom!" he said, but he missed.

I fired my cannon again. "Boom! A direct hit," I yelled and clenched my fists above my head. "Yea! The Americans win again."

On the dusty road, Willie kept his distance from me. I stood on our property between the irrigation ditch and our fence. For several minutes we fired at every vessel sailing past. A fistful of pebbles gave a great rapid-fire machine gun blast at the enemy's ships.

"Hey, Earl, when can you leave your yard?"

"It's supposed to be Sunday, but Doctor Aikens gave us another check-up this morning and said if one of us had caught diphtheria, it would be apparent by now."

Willie's eyes flared. "I went back to the carnival and talked to the black man."

"Yeah?" I said and pitched a rock as far as I could downstream. "Was the black man scary like the Paiutes that come to town to shop at Grandpa Petty's store?"

"At first he scared me, kind of, but he was nice to me. He said he came out West with the 9th Cavalry thirty-six years ago and never went home to Virginia."

"Wow, a Buffalo Soldier!" I said. "Dad said they scared the dickens out of the Indians."

"The carnival is closing down tomorrow night," Willie said. "Do you want to sneak over there and see him? I'll go with you."

"Go where?" I heard from behind me. I turned, and ten feet away, Shirley stood behind our fence, clutching the top rail with her bony arms. She looked like a scarecrow flung against our fence.

"Nowhere," I said.

Little Ruth poked her head out between the middle and top rail. "I want to go!"

"There's a black man at the carnival at the town square," Willie volunteered.

"Why did you tell them?" I said.

"Ooo, I've never seen a black person. I want to go too," Shirley said.

"A black man?" Ruth said. "What made him turn black?"

"He's what they call a Negro," Shirley said. "They have black skin, just like white people have white skin, and Indians have brown skin."

"I want to go, too," Ruth said.

Out of the corner of my eye, I saw Dad walking toward our property. "Hush up," I said, and tilted my head in Dad's direction.

Our dog, Tip, trotted beside Dad with his neck stretched, and his chin held high, staring at a stick which Dad waved in his hand.

"Hey, Tip," I called. Tip darted his eyes at me and continued following the motion of the stick. Dad pitched the stick into the ditch beside me, and like a bullet, Tip raced after the stick. He leaped six feet through the air, crashed into the ditch, and splashed water all over me.

I was happy to hear Dad manage a chuckle.

In a split second, Tip was beside Dad with the stick.

As Dad walked past Willie, Willie took a couple of steps back.

Dad nodded at Willie. "You know you're not to get too close to anyone in our family while the quarantine sign is still on our front door, don't you?"

"Yes, sir, Uncle George."

"We can't be too safe." Dad tossed his stick to me. "Here, keep Tip happy while I tend to water lines across our property."

Tip bounded to me, his brown coat dripping, and his eyes bright with anticipation.

Dad worked his way across our lot, clearing debris from the water line to our cistern and the rows in our fall garden.

Willie stepped to the center of the road and spoke low. "Hey, if Doctor Aikens said you're not infected, let's sneak there and see the black man after I get out of school tomorrow."

"We're still supposed to stay away from people until Sunday," Shirley said.

With the flick of my wrist, I pitched the stick at Shirley. Tip raced after it and skidded against the bottom fence rail and stirred a cloud of dust. I turned my back to Shirley and faced Willie. "Well, I guess we won't be sneaking away to see the black man." I winked hard at Willie, and for some dumb reason, Willie exaggerated a wink back at me.

Shirley hollered, "You're fibbing again! I'm going to tell Mama."

I dropped my head. "Willie . . ."

Tip was back. He panted and danced for another toss of the stick.

To my surprise, Shirley said, "I won't tell if you let me go with you to see the black man."

The town square was two blocks from our house. Sneaking there in broad daylight would be hard enough without Shirley tagging along—she ran like a flapping duck.

I turned and faced Shirley. "All right, I tell you what. You can go with us if you promise to tell Mama and Dad you're not mad at me anymore, and you think it would be okay for me to ride the canal Friday with Dad and Grandpa Spendlove."

"Tell him yes, Shirley," Ruth said, "so I can see the black man with you."

"No, you're too young," I said. "We'll have to run fast."

"Aww," Ruth whined.

I said to Shirley, "What do you say? Do you promise?"

"Uh-huh. But I'll tell Mom and Dad, after, I see the black man."

It was my best hope to ride on Friday. I turned to Willie. "Okay, Willie. Come by here tomorrow after school. Dad will be at the orchard, and maybe Mama will be too busy to miss us. We shouldn't be gone long."

* * *

The rest of the afternoon, I worried Shirley or Ruth would slip up and spill the beans on our plan to sneak and see our first-ever black man. I paid close attention to my sisters' chatter during supper, something I never did before. Ruth was five years old and might not know better—and Shirley was Shirley.

Radio broadcasts were only in big cities in 1926, so in the evenings, we read to each other or played games before bedtime. When Dad was happy before Jennie died, he often took his accordion from the trunk at the foot of his bed, and we sang fun songs and church songs together as a family. He never played the accordion again.

Though she was heartbroken, that evening, Mama stoked the fire in the woodstove and heated two cups of the molasses which Grandpa Spendlove was famous for making. I stood on our stepstool, and with two potholders, I shook a large black kettle and lid and cooked a big batch of popcorn.

Ruth and Shirley sat ready at the kitchen table with their hands slathered in thick, cool butter and a large ceramic bowl in front of each one of them. When the last kernel popped, Mama took her apron in her hand and removed the lid, grabbed the handles, and stepped to the girls.

Mama poured half of the popcorn into each of Ruth and Shirley's bowls. She returned to the stove. The molasses bubbled at a slow boil, and with her apron in her hand, she picked up the pot's handle and hurried back to the girls.

"Watch out, girls," she said. "This is hot." Mama dribbled the dark brown molasses over the popcorn. "There—now mix everything well with your hands and roll popcorn balls the size of an apple."

The gals managed to smear molasses up to their elbows. It was all over the table, and they had splotches on their noses and chins.

Popcorn balls, or pulled molasses candy, were always special treats for us. I ate my share, and the next couple of days, I enjoyed a little more of the sweet molasses I found in Ruth and Shirley's hair.

We enjoyed treats after supper, but it created extra work for Mama. And every night, long after I was in bed, I would hear the clang of Mama putting away silverware and dishes. A short time later, I often hear the wet mop slap onto the wood floors, followed by the soapy water trickling into her bucket as she wrung out the string mop with her strong hands. Mama often said, "I guess I wasn't meant to have pretty hands."

But no matter how late I heard Mama tending to the family's needs, I always smelled breakfast on the table when she woke us early the following morning.

CHAPTER 5   THURSDAY MORNING

While I did my barnyard chores Thursday morning, Mama sat with Ruth and Shirley at the kitchen table and tore narrow strips of cloth from Mama's stash of threadbare hand-me-downs, old bedsheets, and scraps of fabric. With needle and thread, they stitched together the random lengths of material rolled into cloth ropes while on their hands and knees.

Our living room had a wall-to-wall carpet made of rag rope woven on Sister Russell's loom and hand-stitched together to create a carpeted floor covering. We always appreciated the small rag rug in front of the kitchen sink on cold winter days.

I waited and waited for Willie to get out of school, but I no longer heard carnival activity. I feared the arcade booths, concession stands, and tents would be taken down, packed up, and trucked away before we got there.

Every Tuesday and Thursday at half-past three, Dad would walk to our eleven-acre orchard less than a mile from our house, and at four o'clock divert canal water into our orchard's irrigation trenches.

I tried to think of an excuse to stay at home and not accompany Dad to the orchard and sneak to the carnival. And I found my excuse when Dad and I walked out our back door when

I saw the tin roof cowshed attached to one side of our barn and the tool shed attached to the other side.

Orchard farmers wasted no fruit. The best fruit was sold locally or hauled by a freight train as far north as Salt Lake City. The excess and less attractive fruit were peeled, sliced, and bottled, or dehydrated.

Many of the farmers in Hurricane paid the Dixie Evaporator Company to dehydrate their fruit in a hothouse with stacks and stacks of metal shelves, but not our Dad - the hot tin roofs worked just fine. And although our fruit slices fed a million barnyard flies during the drying process, Dad considered the fly-specked fruit perfectly safe to eat because no germs could live on a red-hot tin roof.

I said, "Hey Dad, I can gather the fruit slices on the cowshed roof for you. They should be good and dried."

I put on my sheepish grin and thought I might test the water. "We can take dried fruit to eat when we ride the canal tomorrow—if I get to ride with you. I sure hope I get to ride."

Dad half-smiled. "Your mother and I are still giving it thought. Have you apologized to your sister for shooting her out of the mulberry tree?"

I tried to look pitiful. "Kind of, but she didn't want to listen." "By the way, you've lost your BB gun for two months," Dad said.

"Does that mean I can ride with you?"

"No."

"But you took away my BB gun for scaring Shirley. And not letting me ride the canal is double punishment."

"We'll have a family discussion tonight at the supper table." He looked across the backyard toward the shed and the blanket of fruit slices on the gently sloped metal roof. "Yeah, you're right. It is time for the fruit chips to be gathered. Get the willow baskets from the front corner of the tool shed, and I'll stand the ladder up for you. Shirley gets to hold the ladder—I hope she doesn't let you fall."

For me to take more than two hours to gather the dried slices of peaches, apples, and apricots would be a stretch. If I finished too soon, I might have to go to the orchard with Dad and miss seeing the black man. I swallowed hard. "Maybe it would be nice if I helped Shirley with the dishes first, and then Shirley can hold the ladder." I couldn't believe that came out of my mouth.

"Good idea! You'll look cute in your mama's apron."

"I don't need to wear an apron."

"Sure, you do." Dad motioned and said, "Go to the kitchen— *Earlene.*"

By golly, I set myself up for that, but at least Dad showed some light-heartedness.

* * *

After drying the dishes, I found Dad in the barn. I told him I was ready to gather the fruit. He fetched the ladder hung horizontally on the barn wall. I followed him to where Shirley waited. Dad leaned the ladder against the edge of the shed's roof—maybe seven feet off the ground.

I climbed the ladder to the roof's edge; Dad pitched the three baskets up to me. He sat Shirley on the bottom rung of the ladder and told her when I came down with a basket of fruit; she was to stand behind the ladder and hold it steady. "Earl needs to appreciate you doing something nice for him while he's up high, not like the stunt he pulled when you were in the mulberry tree."

"Can I push the ladder over and leave him up there?" Shirley said.

Dad fought back a smile and shook his head. "You don't want to do that."

"Uh-huh. And I want to throw rocks at him when Earl is stuck up there."

"Shirley, you should want to prove you're nicer than Earl," Dad said.

It didn't worry me, Shirley wanted to throw rocks at me. With the limp noodle of an arm she had, she couldn't hit the broad side of the barn. They must have coined that phrase for her.

I busied myself scooping up the fruit chips. Although it was November, the Indian summer made it uncomfortable to work on the hot tin. It was too hot to crawl on my knees, so I kind of monkey-walked and gathered the fruit chips.

From my vantage point on the roof, I saw Willie with his books strap flung over his shoulder, trotting our way. School let out at 3:15, so I knew it was time for Dad to tend the irrigation lines at our orchard, but he was still in the livery currying the horses, something he always did before he rode a horse any distance.

I called to Dad through the hayloft window above the cow shed's tin roof. "Hey, Dad, don't forget it's time to water the orchard."

Through the loft's window, I saw Dad remove his watch from his overalls. "You're right; I let the time slip up on me. Thank you, son."

"You're welcome."

"Do you need much more time?" Dad said.

"I have another whole basket to gather."

"Well, stay after it. I'll ride to the orchard and water everything."

Dad rode Dixie out the rear corner of our yard toward our farm plot.

A moment later, Willie stood at our side road. I hurried and scooped up the rest of the fruit. "Hold the ladder, Shirley," I said. "I'm coming down."

"Okay, okay, hurry up. It's too hot out here," Shirley said. She held the rails from the backside of the ladder as I scampered down.

"It would be safer for you to stay here and not go to the carnival with us. We have to run fast," I said to Shirley.

"No. You better let me go, or I'll tell."

Rats didn't work. I thought.

"All right," I said. "Let me see where Mama is."

When I neared the back door, Mama stepped out.

"Hey, Mama . . ." I tried to come up with a question to ask. But before I could get my brain in gear to speak, Mama said, "Earl, I need you to watch Shirley and Ruth for a little while. I want to lie down for a short rest while LaDean is napping. Can you do that for me without picking on your sisters?"

I couldn't believe my ears. I had inherited Ruth for our secret journey, but at least I was going to see my first black man.

"Yes, ma'am, I will. Have a good nap."

"Goodbye, Mama," Shirley said.

Oh Lord, I thought. I wasn't aware Shirley followed me to the house. Shirley was the dumbest smart person I knew.

"Goodbye?" Mama said. "I'm only going to the bedroom for a nap." She flapped a hand and chuckled.

I wanted to pop Shirley on the back of her head, but I was already in trouble. "Ha-ha, don't be silly, Shirley," I said. "It's not like anyone is going anywhere."

Before closing the back door, Mama said, "You kids stay outside and don't be coming in-and-out and closing this door while I'm trying to rest."

Ruth scooted around Mama and hopped onto the porch. "Here I am," she said.

"Be good," Mama said and disappeared from the doorway.

I felt weak-kneed, but relieved. "Shirley, you have to hold Ruth's hand so she can keep up with us."

'Okay, but don't run."

"We have to run. Dad may be home in an hour or so. Come on, follow me."

I motioned for Willie to meet us on the back corner of our property.

Still, under quarantine, my sisters and I couldn't be seen in the street, so I planned to sneak along the rear property lines down the center of the blocks to the town square.

"Willie, to be safe, you need to run along the street, so you don't get our germs," I said. "And you can scout ahead of us when we cross the roads."

"Oh, okay," he said.

Willie hung his book strap around our corner fence post and sprinted to the street corner at the intersection of 200 North and Main Street. Once he was in place, he bent with his hands on his knees and stared at us. I waved to him and pointed in the direction we were going. Willie nodded and trotted down Main Street parallel to us as we moved along our rear property line.

"Come on, girls, don't talk, and keep up with me," I said.

Crouched low, we jogged along our fence behind the barn. Beyond our barn, fresh cow patties covered the cow pen, so we climbed through the fence rails and into Brother Ryder's backyard. The knee-high dried and yellowed grass hissed against our legs as we raced through it.

We crossed to the far side of the Ryders' yard. I looked up the property line and waved to Willie standing on Main Street. He waved back, as excited as if he hadn't seen me in a month.

I flung my arm for him to stop waving so someone wouldn't wonder who he was waving at.

I stepped through the fence to Brother Ruesches' yard. A yelping dog approached us from behind. As I looked back, I felt a blunt thud to the side of my head. "Dang it!" I'd smacked my head on the top fence rail.

"Hey, Tip," Shirley said.

Tip leaped through the tall grass, his tongue flapping to the side of his face between yelps.

"Hush, Tip," I said.

Tip danced around Shirley and Ruth, yelping for their approval.

"Hush, Tip. Hush. Good boy, good boy," I said. "Now, be quiet."

Tip's eyes gleamed, he panted and bobbed side to side, so pleased to find us.

I didn't want Tip to tag along, but we didn't have time to take him home, so I stomped my foot and pointed. "Go home, Tip." I tried to look threatening and lurched at him. "Go home!"

Tip slinked back. He knew what I meant but stood his ground and panted.

I scrubbed my head where the fence rail clobbered me. I looked at Tip. "Good boy—stay with us." Tip stepped close and raised his head, and I patted him.

The back half of the next yard, where the Ruesches lived, was planted in apple and pear trees with the ground littered with fallen fruit. "Come on, girls," I said. "Watch your step."

Tip leaped through the fence as I swung my leg over the bottom rail to the other side. The fruit on the ground had soured and fermented. Honeybees and other insects crawled over the soggy fruit. A few drunken bees buzzed around us in loopy flight; others were too drunk to fly.

Shirley crawled through the fence and then helped Ruth through. Stooped, I trotted beneath the tree branches, squishing rotten apples with each step. I stopped to look back and check on the girls.

Shirley took Ruth's hand. Shirley planted her first step on a couple of rotten apples; her foot skidded out from under her. And own she went on her bottom. *Splat.*

Ruth landed beside Shirley. *Splat!*

Both girls squealed.

"Shush, shush," I said.

I ran back and grabbed Shirley's hand and pulled her to her feet. "Don't cry! Somebody will hear you." Without a word, Ruth climbed to her feet. Both girls had crushed a couple of bees in the applesauce that covered their backsides.

I swiped the fruity mess from her fanny as Shirley sobbed.

"Calm down," I said. "Wipe yourself off and let's get going. You're not hurt."

Ruth burst into tears and said, "I want to go home. I don't want to see a black man anyway. I want to go home and be with Mama and Jennie."

"Jennie?" I said. "You know Jennie's not coming back, don't you?"

Shirley bawled. "If she can live in heaven, why can't she come back to live with us here?"

"Please be quiet. I said. "Jennie's an angel now, and we can't see angels. Stop crying. You're okay."

The girls whimpered and sniffed for a few minutes. After they rubbed their eyes clear of tears, I said, "Come on, we need to let Mama have her nap. You'll like seeing what a carnival looks like even if you don't want to see the black man."

Ruth and Tip stood ready to go. Shirley continued swiping her backside.

"Come on—stay close to the fence," I said.

The last of the autumn leaves dangled from the fruit trees, not offering much cover. I studied the back doors of the neighbors' houses and outbuildings.

We scampered across the backyard to the far side of the fence along State Highway 9 and skidded on our knees.

I searched for the best route either side of the rear fence line on the next block. I planned to run to the middle intersecting corners of the four back yards, turn right and run along the two common lots, and from there run across Main Street onto the town square where the carnival operated.

To the left, in the Hall's fence line, fruit trees and a chicken coop stood along the rear property line. And on the right side, in the Wadsworths' property, there stood a pigpen and toolshed. Along the far side of the toolshed, a couple of horses grazed in knee-high grass.

Out of the corner of my eye, I caught sight of the screen door on Sister Hall's house swings open. The closure spring twanged. We ducked down. With the screen door to her back, Sister Hall— in a straight dress and apron down to her ankles—twisted and heaved a washtub of soapy water onto her backyard. The sheet of water slapped the dry ground. I imagined the sizzling sound the suds must have made on the ground. She stepped back inside her house, and the screen door slapped closed behind her.

My mama would never waste water like that. Our used wash water was used to scrub our front or back porches.

No traffic appeared up or down Highway 9. The sun's heat raised fumes from the oil sprayed on the road to reduce the dust. I heard chicks peeping and kids playing somewhere nearby.

A few blocks away, a familiar sound erupted. *Sput, sput, sput . . . tut, tut, tut, tut, tut.* One of the few diesel engine farm tractors in Hurricane cranked up. Since it was November, the diesel tractor probably was mowing a field of dried corn stalks for winter livestock forage.

We scurried across the last fifty feet of the property line and crouched behind the cedar split-rail fence.

Crossing Highway 9 to reach the Wadsworth's backyard, and from there sneaking to the Wadsworths' front yard to cross Main Street would be our most likely chances of being seen.

I whispered, "You gals need to stay close to me when we cross the road. We have to run as fast as we can, you hear?"

Willie lollygagged on the corner. He kept staring in our direction, which made me nervous. He was sure to draw attention to us. I motioned for him to move on.

Leaning out across the bottom fence rail, I said to Shirley and Ruth, "Okay, on three, we'll run across the street."

Tip sensed our departure and leaped out, waiting for us in the road.

"One, two, three!" I sprang through the fence with Ruth close behind. Shirley let out her usual frantic whine, clambered forward, snagged her foot on the bottom rail, and belly-flopped with a squawk. Ruth and Tip made it to the Hall's yard like they were shot out of a gun.

"Get up, get up. Get going," I said while running back to

Shirley.

I dragged Shirley across the street, leaving parallel scuff marks from the toes of her heavy, lace-up shoes.

We hid behind an old wagon bed to slow our hearts and our huffing and puffing. Tip sniffed the side of the wagon and the grass near it. He lifted his hind leg and staked his claim.

"The fence rail hurt my foot," Shirley said.

"You're not hurt."

"You don't know!" Shirley said. "It might be broken for all, you know."

"Come on; you're all right," I said. "We won't run, but walk fast. Ruth, you take Shirley's hand and help her."

I checked Mrs. Hall's screen door. "Come on, let's go."

Apples squished beneath our feet. "Ewe, ewe, ewe," Shirley said.

"Hush!" I whispered.

We trotted past the chicken coop. The chickens fluttered and clucked.

Shirley hobbled like a snared bear.

"Cut it out, Shirley, you're not hurt," I said. "Get back to the fence line."

We crouched and sneaked behind the Wadsworths' tool shed. I forgot there were beehives on the far side of his toolshed. Shirley and Ruth squealed when they saw the humming wooden boxes.

"Don't panic," I said. "Bees won't bother you if you don't bother them." We passed the four white boxes. The worker bees buzzed us.

Shirley's whine climbed a couple of octaves higher.

"Don't slap at them," I said.

We dashed to the intersection of the four lots. Thank goodness no bees followed us. I knelt on one knee, and my sisters did the same. Tip panted and nudged my side for a head rub.

The colorfully painted carnival trucks and trailers were in sight across Main Street. I could hear the clang and clatter of the workers packing to leave Hurricane.

"Oh, wow!" Ruth said. "Look at the pretty trucks. Look at the one with the clown with a red ball for a nose."

"Yeah, and the truck painted with the balloons and the one with the merry-go-round horses," Shirley said.

"Shush," I said.

We needed to slink up the common property line and find a spot in either of the two front yards for cover until it was safe to cross Main Street. I decided the shrub growing next to the large almond tree just inside the Wadsworths' front yard, which fronted Main Street, was the only bush large enough for us to hide in.

"Stay low and follow me to the bush with the yellow leaves, the one behind the almond tree." I checked the back doors to both homes. All was clear. The wind had picked up since morning, and bath towels and bedsheets hanging on the Wadsworths' clothesline fluttered and popped with each wind gust. The forked tree limb pole used to hoist the clothes above the ground swayed with the wind surges.

The two mares in the Pulishers' yard next door stood statue-like, facing the rear fence and keeping an eye on us.

"Okay, now!" I said, and then I darted down the fence line. Ruth and Tip stayed on my heels. Lanky Shirley's arms and legs flailed the air. She pattered three or four feet behind us. Ruth and I ducked inside the large bush. A couple of feet out, Shirley stumbled and piled in on top of us.

"Ewe," Ruth said. "That hurt."

"Shush, shush."

"I didn't mean to," Shirley said.

"Shush, shush," I said.

We untangled from Shirley and caught our breath.

I leaned out of the shrub and peeked to my right and then to my left on Main Street. A brand new automobile appeared, heading our way. It was Uncle Charles. I knew it was him because he drove the only Ford Tudor sedan in Hurricane. The Tudor was a fancier Model T for rich people.

Again, I wondered what Mama and Dad didn't want me to know about Uncle Charles when he visited for Jennie.

He drove past. From the shrub, all I was able to see was his fedora, and his hands hung on top of the steering wheel. The next block, he turned in to a parking space in front of the drug store.

I looked both ways again, up and down Main Street. I couldn't see a car or a horse in either direction.

"Okay. Keep up this time," I said and checked again. "All right, on three . . ."

A rumbling rolled around the street corner. A beat-up farm truck with a driver and a passenger turned onto Main Street and headed our way. The old rattletrap of a vehicle was due a headlight and a new paint job it would never see.

"Wait a minute, wait a minute," I said.

Tip sat calmly and panted.

I whispered to the gals, "As soon as this truck passes, let's run for it."

"Okay," Ruth said.

Shirley whimpered.

When the truck rolled past, I stood ready to run. Ruth and Tip were on the ready, too.

Twenty feet beyond us and the old jalopy skidded to a halt in the middle of the road.

"Get back," I said.

We tumbled into the bush and snapped several branches. Shirley hadn't moved an inch.

The idling truck's engine sputtered. A lanky man on the passenger side opened his door and hopped to the ground. We lay flat and silent. Tip panted in my ear and licked my face. The passenger-side fellow hurried to the tailgate of the truck and reached for something in the bed, but never looked our way. He laughed and held up a gas cap. "Here it is. I told you I didn't leave it at the gas pump." He shuffled to the side of the truck and screwed the gas cap on. The driver laughed and popped the clutch, and the truck lurched forward. The farmhands leaped onto the running board and flung open the door and hopped in. The truck was off and running before he could close the door.

We all sighed. I looked across the street and saw Willie jumping up and down on the carnival grounds trying to get our attention. I held my hands, palms down, for him to calm down and stop acting like a bonehead.

"Okay," I said to Shirley and Ruth. "Just in case we happen to get too close to somebody, cover your mouth and nose with both hands so they can't say we gave them diphtheria cooties." Both girls practiced a cootie cover-up. "That's good," I said. I rechecked the road. "Let's go."

CHAPTER 6   THURSDAY AFTERNOON

We cleared the irrigation trench, darted across the street, and scurried between two trailer trucks parked a couple of feet apart with their loading ramps stretched to the ground. Willie walked to one of the truck's headlights. We nestled down in the deep dried grass beneath one of the trailers. Ruth held Tip against her.

"Where is he?" I whispered to Willie.

"Who?" Willie said.

"Who? What do you mean, who? The black man, that's who," I said

"Oh, oh yeah. I don't see him anywhere! Several trucks have already pulled out for St. George. Maybe he's already gone."

My heart sank.

"I'm not going to tell Mama it's okay for you to ride the canal if I don't get to see the black man," Shirley protested. "That was our deal."

"I can't help if he's already gone." I looked stern at Willie and whispered, "You go ask somebody who works here if the black man has already gone. We'll wait here."

Willie scampered away.

Shirley scrunched her face and waggled her head. "I bet he's already gone."

I balled a fist as if taking aim. "Hold your head still so I only knock a single knot on it."

Footsteps clattered up the loading ramp. The worker's feet scuffed across the trailer's floor above us.

Boom!

The movers slammed the equipment to the trailer floor. The sand and grit on the wood plank floor hissed as equipment was shoved toward the front of the trailer and slammed against the front wall.

Three pairs of heavy shoes traveled in and out, packing carnival equipment. Beneath the trailer, we could see the men's trouser legs as they staged things to load into the van.

Tip flinched with each thud. The trailer's sheet metal walls sounded like a gong when items slammed against them.

What's taking so long? The thundering above us made Willie's absence feel eternal.

"What're you children doing down under there?" a pleasant mellow voice said.

We whipped our attention toward the rear of the trailer. There he was—ten feet away from us. A huge man—a black man!

Looking at him from beneath the trailer made him look ten feet tall. The black man was black. Tiny sweat beads covered his bald head. Shirtsleeves rolled up past his elbows revealed thick taut forearms. We shook like we had seen a ghost! And this was our first black man.

He walked toward us, and when he was five feet away, all three of us slapped our hands over our mouths and noses and became bug-eyed. Tip cowered with his tail pinned between his legs and growled low.

The black man chuckled. "What in the world?" He bent at the waist to look into our faces.

Tip yelped once and darted away.

My voice muffled by my hands, I hollered, "Don't come near us."

"Beg your pardon?" he replied.

Willie's feet pattered to the front of the trucks. "Don't get too close to them, Mr. Lincoln."

The black man still bent, gazed at us. He said to Willie, "These must be your cousins you were telling me about yesterday—the ones quarantined."

"Uh-huh, that's them, Mr. Lincoln," Willie said.

The sun brightened his almond-colored eyes and broad shiny nose. He stood and remained quiet for a moment. "I'm so sorry to hear about your baby sister. I know losing their baby broke your mama and daddy's heart."

I dropped my hands from my face. "LaDean's the baby in our family. Jennie was three years old. It hurts me to see my mama and dad crying so much, and it's the first time I have ever seen my Dad cry. "

A pleasant smile warmed Mr. Lincoln's face. Shirley and Ruth were still frozen with their palms plastered to their faces.

"Jennie?" Mr. Lincoln said. "That was my mama's name. I've never known anyone named Jennie, who wasn't a sweet person."

"Everybody loved Jennie," I said.

Mr. Lincoln nodded. "Moving around with the carnival, I've heard a lot of dreadful stories about diphtheria. Mostly children are dying from it."

Shirley dropped her hands, shifted to a kneeling position, and stuttered, "Is-is-is your name Mr. Lincoln, like President Lincoln on the penny?"

With his gentle smile, he said, "No, Lincoln is my first name. But yes, my dad named me after President Lincoln. I was born in Virginia, not far from Washington DC, shortly after Mr. Lincoln was kilt. My last name is Washington, like the first president."

Ruth crawled closer to Shirley. Shirley cocked her head and said, "Your name is Lincoln Washington?"

"That's right. No middle name, just Lincoln Washington."

"Dang, what a swell name," I said.

Shirley winced. "Mama told you not to use curse words."

I ignored her. "You're the first black man I've ever seen in person."

"Me, too," Shirley said.

He tucked his thumbs under his overall's bib and tugged. "Well, take a good look. You probably won't see another black man in this part of the country for a long time to come." He chuckled. "Between here and Montana, I bet I've seen no more than nine or ten Negroes, myself. In Virginia, there are as many black folks as there are white folks, so I never drew this much attention there."

Flies buzzed around us. "So, a lot of people stare at you?" I said.

Willie interrupted, "Oh, wow, you should have seen the folks here to watch him when they were setting up the tents."

Lincoln smiled big and shook his head. "Out West here, I get that just about everywhere I go." He nodded. "The children are surprised to see their first black man and their mamas and papas tell them to get away and stop staring, but they near break their necks looking back as they lead the children away."

Little Ruth blurted, "What does it feel like to have black skin?"

"Ruth!" I said.

His eyes rolled to the side. "I reckon no different than your white skin—but I have no way of telling." He looked kindly at Ruth. "Some white people don't like me because of my black skin, but I can't do nothing about that—we're all God's children."

It was quiet for a moment, and then Lincoln said, "I best get back to work. You tell your mama and daddy I'll say a prayer for your family and your sweet little Jennie."

Lincoln Washington trotted away. He was a tall man, well over six feet tall, with firm broad shoulders. His faded denim overalls were loose at his narrow hips.

* * *

We crawled from beneath the trailer. "Come on," I said. "Let's get home. Dad won't be long in the field today."

I kneeled at the back end of the trailer beneath the loading ramp. The gals crouched close to me. Willie kneeled ten feet away. I looked both ways on Main Street. At the street corner, Mr. Albert drove his team with his wagon stacked ten feet high with hay across Main Street and clattered out of sight.

"Okay, we'll go home the same way we came," I said. "Willie, you don't have to shadow us. You can go the way you want."

Ruth's forehead furrowed, her eyes narrowed. "We can't leave Tip. Where is he?"

"Don't worry, he knows his way home," I said. "He may already be there."

Water gurgled and filled the irrigation trench on the other side of Main Street. It was the time of day the canal water rushed to the south end of town.

I rechecked both directions. "Come on. Let's get to the bush where we hid before."

Bent at the waist and knees, we charged into the street. Tip appeared from nowhere and ran in front of us, leading the way.

"Yeah, Tip," Ruth said.

As we reached the middle of the street, Tip leaped into the trench. He splashed and played in the rising water.

I flew across the trench and dove into the bush. On my heels, Ruth jumped the concrete channel and ducked into the shrub beside me. Shirley stumbled across Main Street and made no variation in her stride to clear the trench now full of rushing water. One foot after the other plopped down into the water. She screeched but managed to stumble forward and crash into our hideout.

Shirley bawled and said, "My shoes and stockings are soaking wet!"

"No, joke?" I said. "Why did you step in the water in the first place?"

"I didn't see it," she said.

"Didn't see it? Are you blind?" I slapped my forehead and shook my head. "Lord, help us, please."

Sopping wet, Tip joined us in the bush. Ruth giggled and welcomed our frisky wet hound with a hug. Shirley whined and shoved Tip. "Get away from me, you stinky dog." Tip took the shove as play and sprang back for more attention.

"We have to hurry. Follow me." I sprang forward and ran. We gathered at the intersection of the four properties' fences. Tip flopped against Shirley.

"Ewe," she cried. "Get off of me, Tip."

"Hush," I said. I didn't see anyone in either backyard. "We'll stay away from the fence, away from the beehives. Let's go."

We crossed the Wadsworths' backyard lickety-split and fell behind the wagon bed next to the street.

I looked at Ruth and Shirley and whispered, "Don't forget to watch your step so you won't slip on the fruit on the ground."

I wondered why the fruit laid on the ground and spoiled. Fallen fruit was always raked up and fed to the livestock.

"Okay," Ruth said in her sweet little voice.

"Let's just run home around the edge of the streets," Shirley said.

I narrowed my eyes. "Have you lost your marbles? Someone might see us."

Ready to go, I looked over my shoulder to my sisters. "Let's go now."

Ruth and Tip ran stride for stride with me. Behind us, I heard Shirley's wet shoes slapping the ground. I cleared the irrigation trench with Ruth and Tip and sprinted into the street. Halfway across, I heard the familiar Shirley screech again.

Shirley wailed, "It's all your fault!"

I looked back and saw Shirley clambering out of the irrigation water. She stumbled from the ditch and fell on all fours. She struggled to her feet and hollered, "I'm going home the way I want to go."

Before I could say a word, she stomped and squished toward North 100 East Street, turned in front of the Sander's house, and disappeared toward our house. Tip chased after her and followed her around the corner.

"Oh, brother," I said. "Come on, Ruth. We better beat her home and keep her from telling on us."

We didn't look for any of the neighbors as we scampered across the Rouses' yard, laced ourselves through the fence into the Ryders' yard, and scurried to the far side of our barn. We climbed through the fence and into our backyard. Huffing and puffing, Ruth and I stood bent with our hands on our knees.

Once I caught my breath, I said, "We better see where Shirley is."

Ruth and I were halfway to the house when I heard Dad call from the rear gate, "Hey, kids, where are you going?"

I stopped and turned toward Dad. "Oh, just to get a drink of water."

Dad held Willie's strap of books. "Whose school books are these?"

"Uh, I think they are Willie's."

"Why would he hang his books on our fence post? Where is he?"

"He was here—but he went somewhere. He said he would be back later to get them," I said.

"Where did he go?" Dad said.

"Uh, I—here he comes now," I said.

Willie trotted up behind Dad. "Hey, Uncle George. Those are mine." Willie reached for his books. "I have to get home."

"Here, let me hang them on the fence, so you don't get too close to me," Dad said.

"Yes, sir," he said. In an instant, Willie retrieved his books and ran down the street. "Thank you, Uncle George."

Dad opened the gate and closed it behind him. "Woo, with this unusual heat and wind, I'm tuckered out."

Without thinking, I said, "Me, too."

Ruth said, "Me, too."

Dad snickered. "What do you mean? You haven't done anything to be tired from but gather a few baskets of fruit chips. I'll find something to tire you out."

"We'll be fine," I said.

As Dad strolled toward us, Shirley waddled around the corner of the house with Tip following. Shirley froze in place.

Dad halted and placed his hands on his hips. "And where have you been?" He said.

Shirley shuddered. "I . . . I . . . ."

"Never mind what you are about to say, you kids were told not to play in the front yard while we are quarantined."

I stood behind Dad and placed my forefinger to my lips and nodded at Shirley.

"Don't make me fetch a mulberry switch. You play in the backyard or stay in the house." Dad turned to Ruth and me. "Have you kids been in the front yard?"

"No, sir," I said. "Not a single day this week."

"Well, good for you," Dad said. "I'm going to lie on the basement floor to cool down; you kids see if you can stay out of trouble."

It wasn't unusual on summer days when the heat was unbearable, for Dad to come home soaking with sweat and lay on the basement's cool concrete floor to rest and not eat lunch.

"I'll keep an eye on Shirley, so she doesn't get in trouble again," I called.

Dad paused at the door and looked at Shirley, puzzled. She remained frozen at the corner of the house in her wet stockings and shoes.

"Stay out of the ditch water," Dad said. "And don't come inside until you have dried off. It would be best if you don't let your mother see you like that." He stepped into the house.

* * *

Dad came up from his basement cool-down, and Mama was up from her nap with LaDean. A daytime nap was rare for Mama, but she hadn't slept well since Jennie died. From the back porch, I heard Mama and Dad talking about his plan to ride the canal on Friday afternoon.

I stood close to the door and hoped to hear my name. Mama said she wasn't thinking too clearly just yet, and they could discuss it at supper. Dad agreed, and I heard him walk toward the back door. I darted to the mulberry tree where Ruth and Shirley stood bent at the waist, drawing with sticks in the dirt.

"Don't mess us up, we were playing here first," Shirley said.

"Don't forget what you are supposed to tell Mama and Dad at supper."

"What?"

"You aren't mad at me anymore," I said. "And you think Grandpa and Dad should let me ride the canal tomorrow."

Shirley didn't look up and scratched another stick person in the dirt. "Maybe."

"Hey . . . I took you to see the black man, and you promised."

"Hay is what horses eat," Shirley said.

"Don't be funny – keep your promise," I said.

"I saw the black man, but you made me hurry home and made me step in the ditch water."

"That was your fault. Ruth didn't step in the water, and she's a lot smaller than you."

Ruth put a hand on her hip and said, "Shirley, you promised, and you know what Dad says — if you aren't honest, you aren't anything."

Shirley shrugged and continued drawing in the dirt without saying a word.

I walked to the street side of the backyard, climbed and sat on the top rail of the fence. I could reach into the limbs of our almond tree and pick the few nuts left on the branches. From my perch, I watched Dad lead Dixie, his favorite saddle horse, into the barn. In the dim barn light, I could see him moving about, curring his horse. If he were going to let me ride with him, he would also tend to Lady, our smaller saddle horse.

Lady was born a tiny darling and gentle as a lamb. Mama felt a special spot in her heart for the sweet filly and would pat her and say, "How's my little lady, today?" At first, we called her Little Lady. She never grew taller than a pony, and for me, she was just what the doctor ordered.

Twenty minutes later, Dad came from the barn waggling a long straw between his lips. He strolled to the corral where Lady grazed on the last of the year's grass. He stood against the fence, placed a scuffed brogan on the bottom rail, clasped his hands, and rested his forearms across the top rail. His Panama straw hat rested on the back of his head, tilted upward

"Come on, Dad," I murmured to myself. "Please put Lady in the barn for me to ride tomorrow."

As if he heard me from a hundred feet away, Dad looked over his shoulder at me. I pretended to be busy and tugged on the limb above me and reached for an almond.

Dad nodded at Lady. He tossed the straw from his lips and dropped his foot to the ground.

I felt my balance sway backward. I clutched my grasp higher on the limb in my hand to steady myself.

Dad stepped toward the corral gate.

"George," Mama called from the back door. "You and the children wash up for supper. It's not much, but come eat."

Dad barely touched the gate. He dropped his hand and walked toward the house.

Mama leaned out the door and looked at Shirley and Ruth. "You girls come set the table, please."

* * *

Supper was Ruth's favorite: a thick slice of Mama's bread, buttered and toasted, with tomato soup, ladled over it. "Yummy," she said as we took our seats.

Once everyone was comfortable, Dad said, "Earl, will you say the blessing on the food?"

Everyone bowed their heads and folded their arms.

I squeezed one eye closed. "Father in heaven, thank you for the food you have given us and bless it to nourish our bodies for our daily needs. Bless those in need. Bless our family and bless Grandpa and Dad to be safe when they ride the canal tomorrow—and bless me if I get to go, too. We say these things in the name of Jesus Christ, Amen."

Mama and Dad were looking at me when everyone said amen.

Mama stood at her place and said, "The soup is too hot to pass around the serving bowl, so get your piece of toast and pass your plate to me. I'll ladle your soup for you."

I couldn't believe Mama or Dad didn't take my bait to talk about the canal. I knew I heard them say they would talk about it at supper. I glanced at either end of the table where Mama and Dad sat.

I caught Shirley's eyes with my stare. I flicked my eyes and tilted my head toward Mama. Shirley gave me her prissy shrug. I blazed and flicked my eyes again.

"Earl," Mama said.

"Yes, ma'am," I blurted. *Was she giving in?*

She held out her hand. "Get your bread and pass me your plate."

Mama served everyone before serving herself a small portion and sat. Dad looked at her and said, "What did you kids do this afternoon while I was at the orchard?"

I froze, staring at Ruth and Shirley, and they stared at me. I managed to say, "Uh—"

Mama spoke. "Whatever they did is fine with me. I didn't hear a peep from them, and I had the good nap I've needed."

"That was thoughtful of you, kids," Dad said.

"You're welcome," Ruth said.

No one talked much. We were getting close to finishing our supper, and Shirley hadn't offered her forgiveness of me. The canal ride hadn't been brought up. Dad grasped the seat of his chair and shoved away from the table.

"Wait!" popped out of my mouth.

"Wait for what?" Dad said as he pushed his chair farther from the table and stood.

"Are you already through with your supper?" My voice screeched a little higher.

"No, I'm making myself a little dessert." Dad stepped to the counter and took a cluster of red grapes from the fruit bowl. I knew what he was about to do—one of his favorites. Dad returned to his seat, took a slice of bread, broke it up, and dropped small pieces into his half-glass of milk. With his spoon, he churned the bread into the milk. Dad plucked four or five grapes from the bunch and dropped them into the thick, gooey white concoction and shoved them down. He took a big gulp, lowered his glass, and chomped on a couple of grapes. "Aha, that's good."

"Ewe," Shirley said.

I lit up my stare on Shirley again.

She glared back at me.

Ruth caught the looks I made at Shirley, and then volunteered, "Shirley's not mad at Earl anymore."

The way Shirley flinched, you would have thought she had the hiccups.

"Is that true, Shirley?" Mama said. "Has Earl made up with you for being so mean and scaring you out of the tree?"

Dad tilted his milk glass at his face and dug his spoon inside the glass, racking the white goo and grapes stuck to the bottom. He paused and with one eye, peered around the side of his glass and waited for Shirley's answer.

All eyes were on Shirley.

"I guess he was nice to me today," Shirley said quietly, "so I guess I'm not mad at him anymore."

"You guess?" Dad said. "So, you don't know for sure?"

Shirley wouldn't look at me.

"Well, I'm not mad and don't care if you want to let him ride the canal with you," tumbled out of Shirley's mouth.

My chest swelled with a rush of fresh air.

Mama and Dad gazed at each other for a moment. Dad returned to spooning a clump of dessert, clinging to the bottom of his glass.

Chomping his last grape, Dad said, "I vote he rides the canal tomorrow."

Mama thought. She tightened her lips and tilted her head. "It just scares me. If we get rain from the clouds that blew in today, the canal would be dangerous. I'll leave it to you if you feel Earl will be safe."

Dad nodded his head slowly. "With my dad coming along, I'm sure we can handle any situation."

Finally, I knew I was going to ride the canal, but now I was kind of scared.

Dad looked at me. "Earl, finish your supper and then go fetch Lady and lead her into the second stall in the barn. We'll get her ready for you to ride tomorrow."

"Yes, sir!"

CHAPTER 7   FRIDAY MORNING

The wind came in gusts Friday morning. The sky was a flat, gray blanket above the valley and the surrounding hills. I tended to my morning chores and wondered how much stronger the wind must be in the Virgin Narrows along the path of the canal.

Mid-morning, the temperature began to fall. I guessed our Indian summer was giving way to our usual cold November weather. I jogged to the house to get my jacket. When I came through the back door, Mama sat at the kitchen table with a wooden grub box in front of her.

"Burr, I need to get my coat," I said. "It's getting chilly out there."

Mama smiled. "When you go downstairs, go to the storage bin and pick a couple of nice-looking tomatoes and bring them to me."

Unpicked late-season tomatoes tended to stay green while the vines turned brown and wilted, but if we gathered and wrapped them in newspaper and placed them in the cool, dark corner of the basement, they would slowly ripen and be available to eat as late as Christmas some years.

After slipping on my coat, I peeked at several wrapped tomatoes and found two firm red ones. I trotted upstairs and handed them to Mama. She tucked them into a corner of the wooden box.

"There," she said, and replaced the two-board lid and fastened the wire straps tight. "This will feed three hungry men."

I felt pretty big, now that I was going to ride the canal, but thoughts of steep canyon walls crept into my head, and my stomach felt a little queasy.

Mama patted the box. "Sit the box on the back porch for your dad to load up, Earl."

The box was relatively heavy and awkward as I shuffled towards the back door. When I propped the box on my thigh and reached for the doorknob, Mama said, "Finish your chores and come in for an early lunch. You need to spend at least an hour on your homework assignments before you head out with your dad."

Homework was not on my list of things to do, but I nodded and closed the door behind me.

By the time I completed my chores, the wind had settled down, but the sky remained dark. The day before was perfect when we sneaked to the carnival to see Lincoln Washington.

I stepped through the back door. Mama sat at the table, examining Shirley and Ruth's homework. She peered up at me. "Have you already finished your chores?"

"Yes, ma'am. I hurried so I can have my homework done before Grandpa Spendlove gets here."

Mama stepped to the cupboards, sliced two pieces of bread, placed them on a plate, and set it at my place at the table. "Here, eat a little something before you get to your studies." She poured me a glass of milk.

I always loved to slather Mama's apricot preserves on my bread.

After Mama approved the girls' homework, they hopped down and ran outside to play. Mama laid my McGuffey's Reader on the table. I zipped through my reading like a speed-demon and then tackled my math.

"Earl, do not hold your face so close to your paper, and don't bear down so hard with your pencil."

"I'm in a hurry," I said.

"I see, but you're not going anywhere if your work is not neat and correct."

"There. Done," I said and slapped my pencil on the table.

Mama stood beside me and checked my work.

"Earl, Grandpa Spendlove is here," Ruth called from the backyard.

Out of the kitchen window, I saw Grandpa Spendlove ride through our rear gate.

"All right, your work looks fine," Mama said. "Write your name on top of each page, and you can go."

Grandpa dismounted and led Casper, his handsome gray gelding, toward the barn. He lashed Casper to a wagon's wheel and strolled inside the barn to meet with Dad.

At breakfast, Dad told me Grandpa would ride what was called the first leg of the canal while we tended to our chores. The first leg covered four miles of the canal, which ran on the east side of town along the foot of Hurricane Hill. That section of the canal had the control gates to send water in the irrigation trenches across town and out to the farm plots.

Dad and Grandpa Spendlove walked out the barn and led the horses toward our back porch. A sledgehammer and an ax hung from the rear of Dad's saddle. A shovel and a heavy iron pike were strapped to the sides of the other horses.

Grandpa Spendlove was two or three inches taller than Dad. He wore his usual black suit coat and white shirt buttoned at his neck. His broad-brim, a black felt hat, was chalked with sweat stains at the brow. His mustache was thick, and his right eye stitched closed. When he was nine years old playing in the rock quarry, a piece of steel chipped off a worker's sledgehammers and blinded his eye.

I shuffled my reader and papers into a single pile just as Dad poked his head inside the back door.

"You ready to ride, son?" he said.

"Yes, sir!"

I ran outside just as Dad was hanging a box on either side of Dixie's hindquarters. He flipped the stirrups atop the saddle and cinched the girth belt tight.

The stirrups on Lady were drawn up for my short legs. Dad tossed the reins over Lady's head and flicked them behind the saddle horn. He gave me a leg-up to the stirrup, and I grabbed the horn. The leather crackled as I threw my right leg over the saddle. I scrunched into position and shoved my boots tight in the stirrups. Effortlessly, Dad, and Grandpa mounted their horses. I thought of how long I wanted to ride the canal. I felt my knees quiver, and a chill shook my shoulders. But I couldn't let anyone see.

Mama and the girls stepped to the edge of the porch. Baby LaDean slept against Mama's shoulder.

With a shift in his weight and a tug on the reins, Dad brought Dixie alongside the porch. He leaned over and gave Mama a peck on her lips. "Goodbye, Lilly. You gals take care. We'll see you tomorrow afternoon."

"Don't leave us, Dad," Ruth cried. "What if you get killed and can't come back like Jennie?"

Dad paused and furrowed his brow. "I promise you we'll be back," Dad said. Shirley began to cry. "Girls, girls. Please don't cry. We'll see you for supper tomorrow night."

Grandpa dismounted. His lips drawn tight, and his one eye showed sorrow. He said, "Let's share a family prayer and ask our heavenly Father for His blessings and to comfort us all. George and Lilly, if you don't mind, I'd like to offer the prayer."

Dad nodded his approval and climbed down from Dixie. "You stay in your saddle, Earl," Dad said. He held Shirley and Ruth in his arms.

Grandpa spoke slowly. He gave thanks for His blessings and

asked for His Holy Spirit to guide and protect us. We all said, amen. Dad and Grandpa remounted.

We were ready to ride.

"Please be careful," Mama said to Dad. She looked at me with her sweet smile and said, "Earl, you watch after your Dad and Grandpa. We want everyone to return home in one piece."

I fought a quiver in my voice and forced out, "Yes, ma'am, I'll look after them."

"Goodbye, Lilly. Goodbye girls," Grandpa said and held a handheld high. He led us out the rear corner gate; we turned right onto the road and walked the horses alongside our house. Mama and my sisters waved from the back porch. I felt important, and I thought this must be how cavalrymen must have felt when they paraded through towns. I tipped the brim of my hat like the cavalrymen did to the ladies in a movie we saw at Uncle Charles's movie theater.

* * *

Straight ahead was Hurricane Hill, a six-hundred-foot high wall of volcanic rock and sandy soil. After we passed the next block, we turned left onto Highway 9, which was much firmer than other Hurricane roads. Oil was sprayed on them to cut down the dust raised by automobiles speeding past, often full of excited out-of-towners heading to the brand-new Zion National Park.

From the highway, I saw the sloping straight line the canal cut across the base of Hurricane Hill. The canal rose from the desert floor, gradually climbed to the north, and disappeared eastward into the Virgin River Canyon. I swallowed hard.

We steered the horses to the side of the road to let an automobile pass. Dad trotted Dixie up alongside Grandpa. "There she is," he said. "The first thing we'll do is dismount at the headgate and make sure it's working well. Will Hinton replaced the bottom seal last week, and we need to keep an eye on it."

Dad glanced back. "Keep up with us, Earl."

We loped across the city block and turned off the highway. Our first stop was one hundred and fifty yards ahead. We climbed down and tied off our horses. As we walked to the headgate, James Jepson rode his large mule toward us. "Hello, boys," he called in his usual cheerful voice. When he came close, he dropped his smile and said, "George, I sure hated hearing about your little girl."

Dad tightened his lips and nodded. "Thank you, James. It's hard on Lilly and me and our family."

Grandpa Spendlove nodded. "There's nothing fair about it."

"I wish I had the answer for you," Brother Jepson said. "But we won't ever understand all things in this life. But take comfort knowing you'll see your little Jennie again someday."

Dad nodded. His face was pale, and his eyes appeared weak and distant.

Jepson broke the awkward silence, his tone suddenly all business. "Are you boys riding the ditch for Willie Hinton today?"

"Yes," Dad said. "Willie asked me to take care of it for him. He's riding over to Lund's train depot to pick up his mother and father-in-law. They're coming down from Salt Lake to visit and see the grandkids."

"Yeah, I heard." Brother Jepson smiled and nodded toward me. "Is little Earl coming along with you?"

"Yeah—his first ditch ride," Dad said.

Brother Jepson studied me. "Earl, are you up to the challenge? It can be hard work if there's a rockslide to clear from the ditch. The ride itself is no easy task."

He didn't help my nerves any. "I'm a good rider, and I'm helping Dad and Grandpa."

Grandpa Spendlove chimed in. "Earl's up to it. He may be a little on the small side, but he's a small strap of leather, well put together." He tilted his head toward me and smiled with confidence. That made me feel good inside.

Brother Jepson returned the smile and the nod. "Oh, I have no doubt, either. He's a Spendlove, and I've never known a Spendlove afraid of hard work." He turned his mule. "You men be careful," he said and trotted toward town.

* * *

Dad and Grandpa opened and closed the headgate a few times, and were satisfied it was working well.

I was familiar with the canal near town. Every boy and girl in Hurricane played and swam in the channel. It was the perfect place to be on a hot summer day, but I heard about the canal within the steep river canyon was hard work and no play.

When we remounted, the butterflies in my stomach faded. Another hundred yards farther, Grandpa dismounted and inspected one of the canal's five huge cisterns while Dad and I remained saddled. The reservoir was a large, round, concrete holding tank eight feet high and twenty-five feet across. While we waited for Grandpa to walk around it, I asked Dad what the tank did. He said it worked just like the smaller ones in the ground behind our house—it held extra water for when the rains didn't come, and the river dried to a trickle.

My butterflies returned when Grandpa climbed onto his horse. I realized this was it. Our trek into the canyon was happening. We fell into a single file. Grandpa led the way, and I brought up the rear. A few hundred yards out, the trail rose steeply. Lady positioned her rear legs and lurched upward. I scooted forward in my saddle and pressed my knees into her sides. Her back hooves clattered on loose rocks. Dust scattered. A couple of stones tumbled downhill and clicked against other loose stones. Dad glanced over his shoulder toward me.

A cool breeze gusted in my face as we entered the narrow canyon. The canyon's steep walls towered above us, and the grandeur and realization of where I was made me straighten my shoulders. I felt a reverence for the deep canyon, which felt as majestic as a soaring mountain.

Chapter 8   Friday Noon

For the first half-mile, the trail appeared tame. The canal snaked in and out of small gorges darkened by the overcast sky. The canal cut a straight line across the canyon walls of beige and orange earth, sprinkled with brown sage and strips of black volcanic rock. On the canyon floor, spindly leafless trees lined the shallow river.

I often heard tell of the canal's twelve tunnels cut through solid rock, and the six massive timber trestles spanning gullies and deep gorges. We came to the first of the six water flumes. The flume carried water from a canal tunnel to the other side of the gully.

The flumes were big water-troughs, twelve feet wide and three feet deep, constructed of lumber and steel plates supported on wooden bridges which looked like railroad trestles

The dark day made the tunnel look like someone painted a five-foot-high by a five-foot-wide jagged black spot on the solid rock wall. Grandpa once told me it humbled most men when they first saw the tunnels and understood how they were hand-chiseled and dynamited through the canyon's rock walls. Jackhammers and power drills were not available when the men built the canal.

To drill the hundreds of dynamite blasting holes, a three-man rock drilling crew bore the deep holes into rock to set the explosive. Two men knelt and held different lengths of one and one-half inch diameter hardened steel rod with a star-pointed bit on its end.

The driver, the third crewmember, wielded an eight-pound sledgehammer and would strike the top of the bit. The two men holding the bit upright would rotate it one-quarter turn, and the driver would hit the bit again. Again, again and again, the driver hammered the bit, and each time it was rotated until the dynamite hole was bored three or four feet deep into the rock. Some holes took an entire day to bore.

We stopped and climbed off our horses. Dad walked to the edge of the gully, bent at his waist, and rested his hands on his knees. He slowly inspected the timber support posts beneath the flume. The dirt beneath his boots crackled as he slipped five or six feet down the side of the gully to get a view of the underside of the flume.

I became all tingly, and my throat tightened. "Be careful, Dad," I said. "Don't fall…"

"I don't plan to," he said. Dad inspected the flume for leaks and rot.

Grandpa sat on the edge of the canal and slipped into the knee-deep water. "Woo, that's chilly," he said and waded through the steady current. On the far bank of the canal, he found a foothold, grabbed a clump of grass above the channel, and tugged himself out of the water.

Water flew as he shook one pant leg and then the other. Grandpa walked to the edge of the gully, knelt, and inspected the far side of the flume and its support trestle.

Dad's boots hissed against the steep sandy bank. He took hold of the flume and climbed back onto the trail. "A little damp on the underside, but looks good and sound," he said.

Grandpa slipped into the canal, sloshed back across, and

climbed out. "Everything looks good over there, too." Water squished from the eyelets of Grandpa's brogans as he trudged to Casper and mounted. "Earl, saddle up and ease Lady into the canal, and follow me across the flume and then through the tunnel. George, you bring up the rear."

My Adam's apple crawled up my neck as I swallowed hard. I hadn't thought of how we would get to the other side of the gullies and get around the tunnels. Sometimes the water flumes and tunnels were the only paths. "Are we going to ride our horses across the flume?" I said.

"You bet you," Grandpa said.

I gulped again.

"Saddle up," Dad said. "Come on; you can do it."

I clutched Lady's saddle blanket and lifted my left foot as high as I could. I barely managed to get my boot in the stirrup. The good animal she was, Lady stood fast to help me. I hopped up and down on my right foot but couldn't heave myself high enough to grab hold of the saddle horn — *Dang short legs.*

With my left foot hung in the stirrup, I took a couple of deep breaths and gathered my strength, grunted and heaved myself upward. I lunged for the saddle horn, hung in midair for a moment, but felt the smooth leather of the saddle horn slip beneath my fingertips. Downward I went, a pop stung on my backside, and I began sailing upward. With both hands, I grabbed the saddle horn and flung my right leg across the saddle.

Dad stood next to Lady, winked, and turned to mount Dixie.

"Thank you," I said with an unexpected squeak in my voice. I was embarrassed I couldn't do it myself. Usually, I could find a porch, or steps, or a hillside to help me up.

Grandpa leaned back in his saddle and nudged Casper into the canal. Lady took Casper's lead and shuffled down the canal's shoulder into the water. Dad and Dixie followed close behind me.

The current burbled around the horses' legs as we trekked upstream. The hooves against the wood planks of the flume's floor sounded like distant thunder.

The scary thought occurred to me: *This is the first of* twelve *tunnels?*

"Don't be scared," Dad said. "Look straight ahead and trust Lady. She's been here before."

"I'm not scared," I squeaked.

I held the reins in front of me and flared my elbows just a little; the way I knew a true horseman rides. Greenhorns let their arms droop to their sides and rest their hands on the saddle horn.

Lady trudged across the flume. It felt like it would take forever at the pace we made, but I didn't want her to go any faster. The flume spanned forty feet above the gully's rocky bottom. I felt cold sweat on my brow but wasn't about to let go of the reins to wipe it away. *Whew, don't fall, Lady, don't fall.*

The water flume bridged the gully and connected to the tunnel entry. I could see a faint, round patch of daylight at the other end. We were farther up the canal than most kids ever got. We were told to never wade through the tunnel because the bottom was irregular and full of potholes. One time, Willie Isom and I made a torch of dried sage, thinking we would wade through the tunnel. But with our first couple steps, thick spiders' webs snared our faces and stuck like molasses to our hair. Okay, we chickened out—but who knows what kind of snakes and critters hide in a dark place like that?

Telling myself everything was fine, I picked a spot on the back of Grandpa's coat to stare at and trusted Lady to do the rest. Grandpa cleared the flume, but before entering the jagged-shaped tunnel, he halted Casper, drew his leg across his saddle, and stepped into the water.

Lady stopped and fluttered her lips.

I stopped breathing.

Standing in the knee-deep water and stroking Casper's hindquarter, Grandpa smiled at me. "Don't worry, Earl. You stay on Lady. She's not nearly as tall as Casper, and the tunnel ceiling is too low for me to ride through." He chuckled. "I never knew your eyes were so large."

I heard Dad step into the water. "Just watch your head and duck down," he said.

Grandpa tugged the leads, and Casper followed. Ten feet into the darkness, Grandpa, broke into singing his and Dad's favorite song, "Oh Danny Boy." He sounded good in the echo of the tunnel.

"Sing with me, boys," he said.

"I'm not up to singing," Dad said.

Dad loved to sing too, but he hadn't talked much, much less sang since Jennie died. Everyone said he had a good voice, and he often sang at church or performed at town celebrations with a couple of his sisters.

I tried to join in with Grandpa, but Lady stepped into a low spot and stumbled, and I felt a cold chill go up to my legs.

Grandpa boomed, "T'is you, t'is you must go, and I must abide. Will anybody, will sing with me? Earl, we need to sing to scare away any snakes or mountain lions holed up in here."

"Really?"

A chunk of rock on the ceiling struck my head. "Owe." I caught my hat just before it fell into the canal.

Grandpa's voice thundered against the rock walls and ceiling, "But come ye back when summer's in the meadow . . ."

A spider web veiled my face, and I sniffed the sticky stuff up my nose. By the time I managed to peel the sticky web from my face and cautiously open my eyes, the light at the end of the tunnel brightened. It must have felt like what people recount as a near-death experience—a light at the end of a tunnel before they gain consciousness.

Out into the warmer air and daylight, I rode. *Thank you, God.*

Grandpa Spendlove turned and spoke over his shoulder. "You'll have to spur Lady to get back onto the trail." He stretched an arm out and pointed. "There, where the bank isn't as steep—ride up out of the ditch."

Grandpa's boots squished as he trotted out of the canal with Casper in tow.

A cold, stiff breeze from the canyon flipped the brim of my hat. I arched my back and scooted my weight forward, and with a couple of high-stepping splashes, Lady surged onto the trail.

Dad remounted. He booted Dixie's flanks, and she lurched forward, up and out of the canal.

"There," Grandpa said. "We made it without anyone else singing with me."

The wind came from the north, and the temperature fell. We had another couple hours of daylight left.

"Come along, boys," Grandpa said. "Remember to watch for falling rocks, and stay as far from the edge of the trail as you can."

The trail was dry and dusty, and with each gust of wind, the horses' hooves stirred a small cloud that was whisked away down the path.

Casper, Lady, and Dixie loped along as if the steep edge of the trail didn't concern them. I glanced over my shoulder for the comfort of seeing Hurricane one last time, but all I could see was the northern end of Hurricane valley along the Virgin River, where homes were no longer built for fear of the floods.

Grandpa slowed and halted Casper. He waited for us to walk close and stop. He pointed toward the river. "Look down below, Earl, there's LeVerkin hot springs, the Indians called them Pah Tempe hot springs. The Paiutes said the springs were sacred to the Indians, a place of peace to powwow between the many different tribes in the region for hundreds of years before the white man came."

"Oh yeah, you have taken me there before. It looks different from above. The water was hot and stinky".

"That's the natural sulfur many people believe have healing powers. In the cold winter months, when we were building the canal, the workers would go to the hot springs to relax and warm up after a hard winter's day of work. It would make us sleep like a baby."

We approached the next tunnel. The entrance was jagged and crooked. Steel plates formed one side of the canal.

Grandpa stopped and dismounted. He flicked his leather leads in his palm and waited for us. "Everyone walks this tunnel. Fortunately, it's not long, but the ceiling is cockeyed and low. Watch your horse's head and keep a tight lead on the reins to keep her head low."

I studied the depth of the flowing water and leaned to look up through the tunnel. Daylight appeared maybe twenty-five yards ahead.

Grandpa must have read my face. "Don't worry, Earl, the bottom in this tunnel is nice and flat."

I lowered myself to the ground. I watched Grandpa wade into the canal. I placed my first foot into the water. Ooo, it was cold. I tugged Lady and stepped in thigh high. Grandpa pulled on Casper's bridle and stooped to clear the tunnel ceiling. I held Lady's bit and shuffled my feet and felt my way.

When we cleared the second tunnel, we were high enough to peer across the river and see the small town of La Verkin north of the Virgin. The square intersecting streets of the city looked like a checkerboard on the desert floor.

Before there was a town of Hurricane, the men who built the canal lived in the small farming communities of La Verkin, Toquerville, and farther upriver from the cities Virgin and Rockville.

It occurred to me we entered the Virgin River Canyon at river level, and the farther we trekked into the canyon, the higher up the canyon wall the canal climbed. I turned and spoke over my shoulder. "Hey, Dad? How can we be following the canal and getting higher and higher above the river and end up at the river where the water comes from?"

"Think about it, Earl. How can we climb high above the river but end up at the river? That's a riddle for you to figure out, and you can tease your sisters with."

"I don't know. When we left Hurricane, we were fifty feet above the Virgin River. Now we are two hundred feet above the river, but somehow we keep climbing and still end up at the river bottom where the canal gets its water." Then I thought and said, "Wow! There must be a big waterfall ahead."

"No waterfall, but here's a hint," Dad said. "What is the shortest distance between two points?" I turned to look at Dad. He held out his hands and waved his right index finger and said, "Point A, where we left Hurricane Valley." He gestured with his left index finger. "And point B, where the river water enters the canal."

Rounding an enormous boulder which separated the trail and the canal, Grandpa slowed Casper and held a hand toward me. He watched something beyond the boulder for a few seconds, looked at Dad and me, and pressed his index finger to his lips.

"Shh . . ." He held up four fingers and whispered, "Mustangs."

Mustangs!

We moseyed around the boulder and into an open ravine. Just above the canal, on a shallow slope, the mustangs grazed—one dark bay and three painted pintos.

The path widened, and we strolled three abreast. Grandpa whispered, "These old mustangs wander into the canyons this time of year looking for the last bit of sweet grass."

The bay was three or four hands taller than the pinto ponies. The bay snorted. He bowed his muscular brown back, hoisted his black tail, trotted across a small mound, and then turned and faced us. The three pintos continued to graze.

We halted a couple of hundred feet from the closest mustang.

"Oh my, aren't they pretty?" Dad said.

A white mustang with brown patches sauntered to the canal's edge, raised her head, and gazed at us. She bent and drank. Upstream of the horse, the channel flowed from the mouth of a small tunnel, four feet wide at the water's surface and four feet high above the water.

Impatient, the bay pranced and whinnied, protesting our presence. The three pintos scampered past the bay. He swirled around, his glossy coat rippling with powerful muscles as he galloped away.

"What a beautiful animal," Grandpa said.

The mustangs thundered into the canyon. I looked at Grandpa. "I wish we could lasso one and take it home."

He smiled. "That would be one wild and woolly experience. If we chased and tuckered one out and lassoed it, leading a wild mustang out of this steep canyon would be a nightmare. You both would end up at the bottom of the river."

I looked at the river far below. *Dang!*

The next tunnel was jagged and narrow. There was no way we could ride or walk through it, and the trail veered around the large outcrop of lava rock. Dad said the canal flowed through a naturally-formed crevice in the lava rock and saved the canal workers a great deal of work when they progressed to this point.

* * *

We followed the canal and its trail a quarter-mile away from the Virgin River. We crossed a small water flume, waded through another tunnel, and at the farthest point back in the wash, we rode the horses across our third canal flume.

Fifty feet up, the trail Grandpa drew Casper to a halt and climbed down. He brushed back his jacket and placed his hands on his hips. Rock and dirt blocked half the canal channel, and the diverted water eroded the canal's bank and narrowed the trail to three feet wide from the steep drop off.

Grandpa pinched the end of his bushy mustache. "Holy smoke," he said. He turned and gazed at Dad.

Dad dismounted and walked past me, steadying Lady with a

soft pat. His left hand held a shovel. He skimmed his palm across Casper's shoulder as he passed. Standing next to Grandpa, Dad faced uphill, and for several moments neither said anything while studying the debris.

Dad said, "I'll climb up and push the rest of the loose dirt down before we clear the canal."

He walked upstream of the rockslide and found a firm spot to wade across the canal. He spiked the shovel's blade into the steep hillside, and with both hands fixed on the shovel handle, he tugged himself up and stomped his wet boot into the loose soil, probing for a firm spot. Once he managed to get both feet to the height of his shovel blade, he pulled up the shovel, determined another place farther uphill, and sank the shovel into the side of the hill. He repeated the process four or five times before he found a comfortable spot.

Once he was above the spot where the sandy soil and rocks slid from, he used the shovel as an anchor and dug in his boots to prevent sliding downhill.

"Earl, son," Dad called to me, "you'll have to either turn Lady around or get her and Dixie to back up out of the way before I shove the loose dirt and rocks down the hill."

The thought of turning Lady around on a three-foot-wide trail, on the edge of a two hundred foot drop-off, made me want to shriek in fear. "How can I do that?" My voice trembled.

"Lady will help you. Turn her toward the hill," Dad said.

I froze in my saddle.

"Sit still," Grandpa said. "I'll help you. I have to get Casper down the trail, too."

Grandpa grasped Lady's bridle and patted the side of her face. Lady turned nice and slow. Grandpa handed me Dixie's reins. "Stretch your arm behind you and lead Dixie to follow you." Grandpa led us to a broad section of the trail. He fetched Casper and led him to a spot beyond me, Lady, and Dixie.

"All clear, son," Grandpa called to Dad. "Shovel away."

Dad shoved the loose rocks and dirt downward. The sandy soil slid, and large stones first rolled, then skipped and splashed in the canal's water.

"Hold up," Grandpa said. "Let me clean this out, or we'll cause the water to wash away the rest of the canal wall. "

Grandpa waded knee-deep into the water and pitched rocks and boulders over the side of the hill. The larger rocks rolled, clattered, and skipped down the hillside.

"Grandpa, do you want me to help?" I said.

"No, you stay there. It's not safe to have more than one person uphill or downhill. We have to keep an eye on one another."

"Oh, okay." I was glad to hear the reason wasn't that I was too small.

Dixie and Lady shifted their weight and took several stutter steps. I tightened both sets of reins in my fist as the three horses fretted. The narrow trail never bothered the horses before.

Grandpa stepped out of the water and motioned to Dad. "Come on, son, shove some more down." But then he suddenly straightened and froze in place. He slowly stretched a hand at his side back toward me. Staring intently at Dad, Grandpa calmly said. "George . . . Standstill. Don't move."

CHAPTER 9   FRIDAY AFTERNOON

Dad remained motionless. Out of the corners of his eyes, he glanced up the hill.

I thought maybe Grandpa spotted a rattlesnake.

Grandpa said in an even tone, "There's a large mountain lion thirty feet up to your right."

I spied the hillside. There it was. It had to be a male to be so large. His fur blended perfectly with the yellow rocks and dirt. He must have snuck up from the cluster of large boulders. His sharp eyes fixed on Dad.

"Can you shoot him?" Dad said to Grandpa.

"He's too close. If I don't kill him with the first shot, he may attack you."

The lion crouched, extended his neck, and spiked his shoulder blades. As smooth as silk, the cat lifted a front paw an inch and took a short step toward Dad.

Grandpa lowered his hand to his pistol.

The cat flashed his eyes at Grandpa, then back to Dad.

"Let's wait him out," Grandpa said.

The sound of the cold wind from the canyon swirled around us.

A minute felt like an hour. The spooked horses' stammered on the rocky trail and bobbed their heads. Lady snorted.

The lion's nostrils flared, and his chest expanded and contracted with long slow breaths.

A mustang neighed on the distant canyon floor. The mountain lion twitched its ears and broke its stare. The cat glared at Grandpa—then at me.

We waited for his next move.

The cat rose, and his shoulder blades lowered into his muscular back. His trance broken, he turned and trotted up the slope to the cover of large boulders.

Dad and Grandpa remained frozen for another few seconds.

Grandpa took a deep breath and dropped his hand from his six-shooter. "Woo, that'll make you break a cold sweat."

Dad stroked his face and took a deep breath. "How big was he?"

"Plenty big," Grandpa said. "Probably close to two hundred pounds. One of the largest I've seen in years."

Gazing to the spot where the cat disappeared, Dad said, "If he's that big, he's feeding on more than rabbits and ground squirrels."

"You are right about that," Grandpa said.

Everyone took a deep breath.

Grandpa looked at Dad and motioned for him to keep going. "Come on, George, let's get this done. We are going to run out of daylight." He looked across his shoulder toward me. "Earl, you keep your eyes out for our visitor and tell us if he shows up again. Give us a holler if you see anything moving above us."

Dad peered over his shoulder once more and resumed shoveling the loose dirt and rocks downhill.

The work continued. After Dad cleared the last of the loose dirt and rock from above the canal, he climbed into the canal water and helped Grandpa shovel out the debris.

To bind loose spots in the canal's wall, Grandpa and Dad waded upstream a short distance and snatched fists full of tall dried grass which grew on the uphill side of the channel. They returned and worked the straw into the loose dirt with their hands and then tramped the mixture into the weak spot, the same technique early pioneers used to make adobe bricks to build their first houses in southern Utah.

* * *

Underway again, we repeatedly glanced uphill for the mountain lion. Movement below at the river bottom caught my eye.

"Look, there're the mustangs again," I said, pointing down to the river. "I didn't see the large bay down there."

Dad stood in his stirrups and scanned the river bottom. "He's probably not far; mustangs stay in tight-knit herds."

A wind gust carried a hint of the sweet smell which comes before a rain. In the desert, any moisture smells sweet.

Grandpa pulled Casper to a slow walk, leaned to his side, and looked toward me. "Let's water the horses here. Strong winds like this will dry them out."

The edge of the trail dropped-off three hundred feet straight down. I leaned to my right side, toward the hill, and locked my hands to the saddle horn. I probably bruised Lady with my knees.

"Let's water them someplace else," I said with a tremble in my voice.

Still twisted toward me in his saddle, Grandpa's thick gray mustache widened with his smile. "There's a spot in the next gully where we can stretch our legs."

"Let's do that," I said.

With his hand resting on his saddle horn, Grandpa stood in his stirrups and repositioned his weight in the saddle. "That won't be a problem—come along, Little Man." He flicked his knees against Casper, and his horse picked up the pace.

Little Man? Wow, I liked that. I was small for my age, but Grandpa made me proud of riding the canal. Now he was calling me Little Man.

* * *

The turn in the trail was another shallow cove. Grandpa drew Casper off the path. Dad and I rode up alongside him.

"We'll stretch our legs here and water the horses," Grandpa said.

Dad climbed down and offered to help me off, Lady.

"I can do it by myself," I said.

Dad lowered his hands and stepped back. I felt Grandpa and Dad's eyes on me. It felt like the eternal moment you feel when the Sunday school teacher asks you to stand and read scripture aloud in front of the class.

Neither Dad nor Grandpa said a word.

I clamped my hands to the saddle horn and slid my right leg across the back of my saddle. My right foot dangled six inches above the ground. I hung there for a couple of seconds before I decided to release the saddle horn and feared I might fall on my backside.

In free fall, my left foot hung in the stirrup, and I could see myself dangling there, embarrassed. The instant my right foot struck the ground, I sprang up to dislodge my left foot. I clawed the saddle blanket to keep from stumbling backward. *Thank heavens that worked!*

I tried to act nonchalant and avoided eye contact. I confidently popped a couple of firm pats on Lady's rear end and said, "Good girl, Lady. Let's get you some water."

Out of the corner of my eye, I saw Grandpa grin.

Lady lapped water like she was as dry as a bone. I set my mind to my Dad's riddle: *How can we start at the river and ride high up the canyon wall, be hundreds of feet above the river, but end at the river on the far end—and something about point A and point B.*

I spotted a beautifully smooth black rock the size of a silver dollar. I plucked it from the canal and rubbed my thumb across its slick surface.

Grandpa laughed. "Earl, you're a rock hound just like your Dad was when he was your age. Can't help but keep your pocket full of nice-looking rocks."

"I believe he's worse than I ever was," Dad said. "Between the old volcanoes, river canyons and meteorites, southern Utah is a rock hound's heaven on earth."

"And all the neat Indian spearheads and arrowheads, too," I said. And the moment I shoved my new find into my pocket, I saw a pea-sized piece of pyrite, fool's gold, at the edge of the canal water. I grabbed it and shoved it into my pocket.

* * *

Soon we were back on our horses and heading farther into the canyon. I looked at the canyon rim above and then glanced at the river below. The steep drop off made me woozy.

Grandpa slowed his horse to check a wet spot above the canal. Lady stepped close behind Casper just as he swished his tail to shoo away a hungry horse fly and swatted Lady in her face.

Lady lurched and nipped Casper's rear.

Casper whined and bucked at Lady, barely missing her.

Every muscle in my body tightened.

"Whoa, now," Dad said, "Take it easy, Lady. Earl, gently tighten your reins."

Grandpa spurred Casper and separated the horses.

"Don't be frightened," Grandpa said. "These old horses have ridden mountain trails all their lives. They don't want to fall any more than you do."

* * *

The deeper into the narrow canyon we rode, the fainter the sunlight became. Late afternoon sunlight cast a bright amber band across the upper thirty feet of the far side canyon rims. The walls beneath the edge faded to gray and colorless.

Around the face of the hill, we trekked into a large wide opening. The gully was large enough to be another canyon and intersected the Virgin River Canyon from the south.

"Wow!" I said. "What is this place?"

"The Chinatown Wash. The largest of the canyon's gorges up to the dam." Dad said. "Look below; there's Chinatown campsite you have heard so much about."

Chinatown came up in most of the stories canal diggers told. The men set up an equipment repair and cook camp there and ate and slept there.

"This is where we will camp tonight," Grandpa said.

Following Grandpa's lead, we eased off the canal trail and rode down a well-worn switchback trail to the old campsite.

We hurried to set up camp for the night. The grub boxes and hand tools were quickly removed from the horses and set aside. Dad and Grandpa spread a heavy canvas tarp across the ground and strung a second tarp to create a lean-to shelter. Grandpa slipped his saddle from Casper, and Dad stacked our saddles close to where we would lay our heads to sleep.

"Earl, Dad said. "Get busy and gather as much firewood as you can."

I rushed about the canyon floor, gathering dried sticks and limbs deposited on the river's edge. Breaking thicker branches required a firm two-handed grip and a forceful stomp with my boot. A couple of times, I stomped hard, and the branch flexed like a spring, snapped from my hands, and slapped the ground with a thud.

With a match, a fistful of dried grass, and a few slow puffs of breath, Grandpa soon had crackling yellow flames leaping through a white puff of smoke. Just like how my *Boys Life* said to light a fire.

Gradually adding twigs, in less than a couple minutes, he was stacking sticks like a teepee above the fledgling fire. A healthy fire soon raced up through the longer lengths of firewood.

Firelight flickered on Dad's face. He sat on the grub box, leaning with his forearms resting on his thighs. He gazed into the yellow and orange flames, expressionless. He slowly closed his eyelids and paused there. He was someplace else in his thoughts.

The canyon quickly turned dark. I studied Grandpa Spendlove's rugged face and the dark shadow where he lost his eye. He looked the face of a weathered farmer and cowboy.

"Grandpa?" I asked. "Did your parents farm and tend to animals in England?

While poking the fire, he said, "Oh no. The Spendloves and Isoms worked factory jobs, and when they joined the Mormon Church, they moved to this country straight away. When they arrived, they had little money and found factory jobs in New York and New Jersey. They worked and saved enough money before they could head west to Utah.

"But when they reached the Salt Lake Valley, there were no factory jobs for them, and they had no choice but to learn how to farm and raise pigs, cows, and chickens in a parched desert. England and Wales were lush and green. They had faith; it was the Lord's plan for them to move west and to live among the Saints."

The temperature dropped quickly. We grabbed our heavy coats and snugged our hats to our ears. Grandpa freed a thick log from the underbrush and rolled it next to our fire for a bench to sit on. I sat next to Grandpa.

Grandpa placed thicker sticks of wood on the fire. "Let's build a fire to create plenty of hot embers needed to cook. George, what did Lilly pack for us for supper?"

"You know, I didn't think to ask her, but she has never disappointed us. Let's see."

Repeated gusts of wind made the fire roar and spew waves of sparks into the air. I felt a cold sting to my nose and cheeks, and I could see my breath. I heard taps on my hat and shoulders. White beads streaked down in the firelight. Dad secured the lid on the grab box.

"It's sleeting, boys," Grandpa said.

In a clattering white shower, the ground covered with ice pellets.

"Sleet usually doesn't last long," Dad said.

And just like that, it stopped. The white blanket of sleet brightened the dark canyon.

"Wow! I wish it would snow so we could throw snowballs," I said.

Grandpa chuckled. "Let's not wish for that tonight."

The sky lit up and rumbled, and in the distant, white and amber lightning illuminated plumes of thick black angry clouds. The wind suddenly stilled, and pea-size raindrops thumped me.

"Oh my Lord, it's going to rain," Grandpa said.

Like the sound of a sack of dried beans spilling onto a wooden floor, rain showered down on us.

Grandpa climbed to his feet, gathered his saddle and blanket, and shuffled toward his horse, favoring his right knee with a slight limp. He called, "George, It looks like this may be heavy rain. I better turn out the canal. You stay here with Earl."

I sprinted to take cover beneath the lean-to.

Grandpa flung his saddle blanket and saddle onto Casper in one motion and cinched tight the waist belt.

"No, you stay here," Dad said. "I'll turn out the canal."

"No, son, I'll be fine." From his saddlebag, Grandpa pulled out his long duster, unfurled it, and slipped it on. He climbed into the stirrups.

Smoke bellowed, and cinders hissed and popped as the cold rain drenched the fire.

Grandpa turned Casper with the reins and kicked his flank and disappeared into the blackness beyond camp.

Holding the brim of his hat, Dad ran toward the canvas shelter. He scooted beneath the tarp and flung water from his sleeves. He removed his hat and slapped it across his thigh a couple of times. "Oh, boy, what a mess."

Rain roared on the canvas above us for several minutes and then slowed to a drizzle.

"Do you think Grandpa will be all right out there by himself?"

"Oh sure, he will," Dad said. "He knows this canal like the back of his hand."

"What did he mean by the turn out the canal?"

Dad fiddled with lighting a kerosene lantern. "At the dam where the river water enters the canal, there's a spillway to divert the water away from the canal when the river rises quickly and prevent the canal from flooding its banks and wash away its walls."

Rain doused our campfire, and just in the nick of time, Dad managed to light the kerosene lantern. He stretched out on his side and propped his head by holding his cheek in his palm. I sat hugging my shins while resting my chin on my knees.

The rain rustled with the wind and intensity on the heavy canvas tarp above us, making it at times difficult to hear each other. I gazed at the yellow flame swaying from the lantern's braided cotton wick.

The rain eased and finally stopped. The ground, parched bushes, and grasses soaked up the fresh rain. The night critters came to life, creating a commotion of random clicks and chatter.

Moonlight peeked through patchy clouds drifting westward.

I tried to think of something to break the silence with Dad. But then Dad said, "The only thing predictable about the weather in southern Utah is it's always unpredictable. What's the old saying? If you don't like the weather now, just wait a few minutes."

"I've never heard of that before," I said.

Dad smiled. "I bet if it were ten degrees colder, we would be throwing those snowballs you wanted."

The clouds sailed away, and the half-moon came into full view. Moonlight sparkled on the tips of the tall grass and leaves.

I looked toward the canal above us. "I hope Grandpa is okay."

"He's fine, and now the moonlight will help him."

A spine-piercing angry shriek ripped the night air. I flinched.

"What was that?" I whispered to Dad.

He held his hand up for quiet and cocked his head to listen. "Maybe it's the mountain lion we saw earlier today. They prowl at night."

"Where is he?" I whispered.

"Up above us . . . sounds like he's on the canal trail."

"Grandpa's up there!"

A pistol shot cracked above us.

Dad rushed to his feet. "Stay here; don't move." He snatched his gun and holster from beneath his saddle.

I clenched my shins and rocked back and forth. "What are you going to do?"

"I'm not sure, but I want my gun in my hand in case the mountain lion pays us a visit."

"What about Grandpa? Do you need to go help him?"

Stooped over beneath the tarp, Dad strapped on his holster. "I'm not going to go parading around out there in the dark and have your Grandpa accidentally shoot me. We have this one lantern, and I can't leave you here all alone."

In a quick motion, Dad flipped the cylinder open on his pistol and made sure all six chambers were loaded.

He stepped from beneath the tarp and listened for a moment. "Come on, Earl; let's see if we can't get the fire started again."

Dad raked a stick through the smoldering ashes and found a few hot embers. He walked over and reached under our ground tarp, pulled out a large wad of dried grass, and lit it from the hot embers. In a few moments, the damp firewood hissed from the leaping flames with occasional steaming whistles and pops.

I was plenty toasty in front of the fire. But the wet log I set on soaked through to my drawers, which was pretty uncomfortable.

Dad gazed at the bright moon, hung in front of a billion stars. The mist of his warm breath puffed and disappeared in the night air.

I said, "Do you think Grandpa is okay?"

"Oh, sure. With the echoes in the canyon, it's hard to tell how far away he was when he fired his gun, but I imagine he'll be back any time now."

"Do you think he shot the big mountain lion we saw today?"

Dad turned his gaze to me. "Both sounds came from the same direction—he may have."

Another big cat-like scream sliced the night air.

The mountain lion's shrill was enough to curl your toenails. I had heard the angry screeches of house cats and bobcats, but they didn't come close to the mountain lion's squall.

Dad stared at the heights above us. I flinched as a chill streaked through me. I didn't want my back to the canyon wall where the mountain lion hid, so I jumped to my feet. "We need to find Grandpa!"

"Grandpa can take care of himself."

"What if he shot and missed, and the mountain lion attacked him?"

Dad tugged me to his side. "We don't know what Grandpa shot at. It could have had nothing to do with the mountain lion. And if he wounded the animal, we don't need to be out there in the dark. I'll call him." Dad holstered his pistol; he curled his hands to his face and hollered. "Dad, can you hear me? Are you out there?"

The insects paused for a few seconds. There was complete silence.

"Dad, hello. Dad!" he yelled.

Silence.

I shivered, and my teeth chattered.

"Let me try this; this will carry better," Dad said. He hollered as he did when he called the cows to come feed. "Whooooo-wee, whooo-wee."

"Why did Grandpa only shoot one time?" I said. "He should have shot the dumb mountain lion a bunch of times."

"Don't get yourself worked up. There's no way for us to know what he shot at." Dad pointed to the log-bench near the fire. "You need to sit down and try not to worry."

"Dad, why don't you just shoot up where we heard the mountain lion?" I said.

"That's not a good idea, Earl. What if Grandpa is near, and I accidentally shoot him?"

"We have to do something." I shifted my weight from side to side and strained to see anything in the dark.

"Wait—that's all we can do. Sit still and get warmed up."

Dad called out again. "Whooooo-we, whooo-we. Dad, are you out there?"

"Shoot your gun into the air. Grandpa may hear it and maybe you'll scare away the mountain lion, too."

Dad looked at his pistol. "Good idea, son. I should have thought of that." He held his arm straight up. I squinted and placed my hands on my ears. Dad snapped the trigger.

Bam!

Yellow and orange flames flashed from the barrel. Dad looked around and fired again.

Bam!

"That's enough for now," he said. He flipped open the cylinder. Smoke escaped from the spent shells. He quickly reloaded the two bullets.

In the distance, two gunshots popped.

"It's Grandpa," I yelled.

"I'll be," Dad said. "It sounds like he's farther away than I thought."

"Aren't you glad I told you to fire your gun in the air?"

"You must be a better Scout than I give you credit." He looked upstream into the canyon. "If the canal trail was dry, it's better than a half-hour trek to the dam from here, and Grandpa still would need time to work the canal's switch gate. And now, with a muddy trail, I figure it'll be another hour before he returns."

Dad sat on the log next to me. He straightened his right leg and shoved his hand deep into his pants pocket. He removed his watch and tilted its face toward the firelight. "It's eight forty-five. We can expect Grandpa here between nine-thirty and ten o'clock."

I still thought of Grandpa alone in the dark. "I'm glad the mountain lion didn't get him."

"I would be telling a lie if I said the thought never crossed my mind. And it sure makes me wonder what he shot at the first time."

"Maybe it was another mountain lion," I said.

Dad shook his head. "No, mountain lions are territorial; you won't find two big cats snooping around close to each other."

Dad shoved the timepiece into his pocket. "You know what, son? With things happening so quickly, we weren't able to get around to eating. I'm starved—how about you?"

"Me too!"

Dad fetched the grub box and carried it to the fire. He sat next to me and unfastened the wire, which held the lid closed.

We chowed down on Mama's corn beef hash, and sweet sorghum and biscuits warmed by the campfire.

All was quiet, and the wind subsided. The time approached when we expected Grandpa. At nine-thirty on the nose, we heard him call to us from the dark canal trail above our camp.

"George . . . Earl, I see you boys are still awake," Grandpa said. "I didn't know if you would wait up for me."

He didn't know there was no way I could have slept.

"We're here waiting on you," Dad said. "Come on down."

We couldn't see him well since our eyes were used to the firelight. We followed his voice as he wound his way down the trail. "I hope you have something good and warm for me to eat. I haven't eaten anything but a handful of pine nuts since my lunch. I bet Earl has eaten all of my supper."

"We'll find you some scraps," Dad said.

CHAPTER 10   FRIDAY NIGHT

The switchback trail took Grandpa a few minutes to descend to Chinatown camp. As we waited, I realized the excitement distracted Dad from his grief for Jennie. I thought of Mama with Shirley, Ruth, and baby LaDean at home, but Jennie wouldn't be there. She was always happy, asked a thousand questions and loved to be read to.

Grandpa arrived at the far side of the swollen creek from out of the wash. The campfire illuminated his face, Casper's hooves, and the tack hardware.

I jumped up to greet him. "Hey, Grandpa!"

Grandpa surveyed the rapid water and both banks for the safest place to cross.

Dad walked around the fire to the near side of the creek. "I believe that spot is as safe as you'll find to cross. It's no more than a couple feet deep."

Leaning to his side and peering around Casper, Grandpa flicked his stirrups. "Come on, boy, let's get across."

Casper made easy work of the ten-foot crossing and trotted onto our side of the creek.

"We heard you fire your pistol. What was that about?" Dad said.

Suddenly, a few feet downstream, at the water's edge, a cluster of thick bushes rustled, and a flash of yellow beast darted out. The big mountain lion streaked to the canyon wall, vaulted upward and vanished into his dark rocky hideout.

"Iiiiii!" I shrieked. The lion's flight was such a blur; it didn't appear real.

Dad drew his pistol but wasn't quick enough to fire a shot.

"That's some bedfellow you boys were keeping," Grandpa said while steadying Casper. "I wonder how long he had been there."

Dad didn't speak for several moments; he puffed breaths of warm moist air. I shivered to think the cat had been so close and watching us.

Dad glanced at me. "Holy cow."

"W-we need more firewood," I said.

After shaking off his scare, Dad said, "We heard your gunshot earlier and the mountain lion's snarl. Did you wound him?"

"No, I fired to scare him away. Not far up the trail and heard something thrashing loud and frantic in the canal. I halted Casper and saw one of the mustangs trapped in the canal from a hill slide. I caught sight of the big mountain lion slinking toward the mustang. I hollered and broke his trance. When he glared at me, I fired into the air. That's when he screeched and ran away."

"Was the mustang able to free itself from the canal?" I said.

"No such luck," Grandpa said. "I lassoed him and tried to help pull from the soggy mess he churned up, but there wasn't much I could do, so I rode to the dam and diverted the water from the canal. The poor creature was mired near chest-deep when I came back down the trail. There was no way I could free him by myself. We'll have to try again in daylight when we can see."

"What if the mountain lion comes back to eat the mustang tonight?" I said.

"I hope not, they usually don't prey on horses," Grandpa said. "But it is a possibility. The mustang is defenseless, and nature can be cruel."

"Why didn't you shoot the mountain lion when you had the chance?" I said.

"I aimed, but at the last second, it occurred to me the mountain lion was doing what comes naturally to him. We're in his backyard. And after all, we wouldn't want a possibly wounded cat angry in the dark of night."

Visions of the struggling mustang attacked by the ferocious mountain lion swirled in my head—and then a worse thought occurred to me. I blurted, "What if the mountain lion comes back to attack us?"

"Don't worry, Earl," Grandpa said.

Dad said, "We'll tie the horses to the corners of our shelter, and if the cat snoops around, they'll spook and let us know."

"Will both of you sleep with your guns?" I said.

"We'll keep our pistols by our sides," Dad said.

I felt a little safer.

Grandpa ate his supper while Dad and I gathered a heaping pile of firewood.

Grandpa pitched branches on the fire. "Let's get us a good fire to warm us before we hit the hay and hopefully have enough embers in the morning to start another fire."

With a rope strung around our camp and the horses in place, we settled into sleep. I lay between Grandpa and Dad. They insisted I not sleep in my boots, coat, and top shirt so I would have something warm to put on in the cold morning—but I wasn't about to take anything off in case we needed to run from the mountain lion.

Dad and Grandpa laid their pistols to their sides at arm's length. Two heavy wool quilts spread across the three of us.

I was warm and toasty.

I closed my eyes, and I tried to go to sleep. But I heard the sound of every creature and critter for miles and the distant baying of wolves. Often the dying fire popped and crackled. The cold night air made my face tight and tingly. I tugged the quilts over my head, but soon my breath overheated the air underneath. I came up for fresh air every so often and heard the creepy sounds again.

Finally, I squirmed on to my side, and my shoulder held the quilt away from my face. It gave me my best combination of warmth and fresh air.

I must have fallen asleep, but I stirred when Grandpa and Dad broke into choirs of severe snoring. For a while, they snored in unison, and other times, they snorted alternately, sounding like a two-man crosscut saw ripping through hardwood.

I nudged Dad and Grandpa. I called their names. Thankfully, Dad rolled to his side and only breathed heavily.

Grandpa then seemed to snore louder. I found myself breathing in rhythm with him. And then for a moment, he stopped breathing. I found myself struggling for breath and mentally coaching him to *breathe, breathe*.

Seconds before I blacked out from lack of oxygen, Grandpa snorted loud, and his whole body flinched, and we both began breathing again.

Time crawled. I thought I would never sleep.

CHAPTER 11   SATURDAY MORNING

Daylight appeared on the edge of my quilt. I heard sand crackling beneath Dad's and Grandpa's boots. I pried open one eye and saw them standing with their backs to a golden crackling fire. The temperature was near freezing, and frost glazed the brushes and grasses. The crackling and popping of the campfire were comforting, but I felt too warm and comfortable to get up.

Dad and Grandpa spoke in low tones. My breath rustled against the quilts. I remembered the trapped mustang, and my fear for its fate jolted me to get moving.

I shoved the heavy, warm quilts to the side and struggled to my feet. "When are we going to free the mustang?" I said.

"Hey, look here," Grandpa said. "Earl did plan on getting up sometime today."

By the time I walked to the fire, I was trembling, and my teeth chattered. A bright band of morning sun crept down the far canyon wall. The morning air was fresh and crisp.

"See," Grandpa said. "If you hadn't slept in your coat and boots, you would have something nice and warm to put on this morning."

I shivered too hard to talk, and they both laughed.

Dad tugged me against him and stroked my shoulder. "We'll

get a hot breakfast in you. That should get your motor running."

Dad flipped open the grub box and removed a beautiful slab of heavily salted side meat pork wrapped in flour bag cloth, several eggs, bread, three apples, and two shiny red tomatoes.

"I was starving, I said.

Grandpa opened another wooden box and produced three feedbags partially filled with oats and strapped them onto our horses. Steam rose from the three animals as Grandpa curried their glossy coats.

With a long sharp knife, Dad sliced the slab of side meat into nine thick slices. Each slice crackled and then wrinkled when laid in the cast iron skillet. The sizzling pork fat smoke smelled oh so good.

Dad placed the cooked meat on a plate and poured most of the hot grease to the ground, set the skillet on the ring of rocks, and proceeded to crack open a half dozen eggs. His fork pinged on the black iron as he whipped the eggs. He dashed in salt and pepper and tossed in a chunk of butter and whisked it all together. The eggs changed from liquid gold in color, to fluffy yellow. Dad picked up a tomato and the sharp knife.

"Are you going to bless the food you prepared for us, George?" Grandpa said.

Dad's eyes filled with tears. "I don't feel like giving thanks to anybody."

"I understand. I'll offer a little prayer for us." Grandpa said, and his blessing was short and simple.

"Dig in, Earl," Grandpa said.

"No, wait a minute, wait a minute," Dad said. He held the knife to the tomato. "Here, Earl, try a slice of this. You won't believe how good sweet tomato taste on your eggs."

I gave a fearful groan. "Sliced tomato on scrambled eggs?"

"Oh, you bet you," Grandpa said. "Here, give me several slices of tomato, George."

Dad and Grandpa covered their eggs with slices of tomato.

Trying to act grown-up, I held out my plate and asked for tomato on my eggs. And howdy, it was delicious! One of the best things I had ever eaten.

I chowed down and put away my breakfast without coming up for air. Dad and Grandpa chatted and took their time. They acted like they had forgotten the poor mustang stuck in the canal. I didn't want to make them mad at me, but I had to say something to prod them. "I hope the mountain lion didn't come back for the mustang last night."

"Oh, we would have heard a terrible commotion echoing off these canyon walls had the mountain lion returned for the trapped horse," Dad said.

"We'll head up the trail as soon as we break camp," Grandpa said. "You should have slowed down and enjoyed your breakfast."

* * *

The horses snorted steamy puffs of breath as they trudged up the switchback from the bottom of Chinatown Wash. When we reached the canal trail, the bottom of the empty canal was muddy with shallow puddles.

A quarter-mile up the trail, Grandpa, leaned, and spoke to us. "Around this bend, we should find our mustang."

Sure enough, rounding the bend, I saw the beautiful mustang pinned in the canal, mired in thick mud to the underside of his chest. The animal must have been between the hillside and the channel when the bank collapsed and forced it into the ditch.

We dismounted. Grandpa cautiously approached the mustang and surveyed the situation. The horse tugged against the pool of mud, but it was weak and helpless.

"What a difficult situation we have here," Grandpa said. He turned to Dad. "What do you think, son? How are we going to free this animal?"

Dad shook his head slowly.

"We have to get him out of there," I said.

"Oh, we'll get him out," Grandpa said. "We have to get the water flowing through the canal one way or the other."

"What if we can't?"

"Worst case, we may have to put the horse down and quarter him so we can dig him out."

I choked. "You wouldn't do that, would you?"

"That's the worst of possibilities," Dad said. "One way or the other, we have to restore the water flow. That's the ditch rider's number one responsibility."

Grandpa strolled to Casper and removed a rope and a shovel. "Let's get to work."

Dad retrieved his rope and a shovel. I felt important as I removed my rope from my saddle, too.

The portion of the canal where the mustang was trapped was a natural shelf in a crook in the canyon wall. The horse faced toward the canyon with its hindquarters to the hill slope. That was lucky—the empty canal's bottom would have been too muddy to get in and try to tow the mustang upstream or downstream.

Dad shoveled mud from in front and to the side of the frightened mustang. The animal neighed and tried to bite Dad. Its lips and nostrils caked with dried mud.

After little success, Dad trudged from the ditch and stomped mud from his trousers and boots. Grandpa stepped close to the horse He spoke slow and gently and stroked its neck. He looped two lariats over the horse's head. With earned trust, Grandpa brushed the dried mud from the mustang's snout.

Grandpa said, "This horse could suffer a heart attack if we don't wet-him-down and get water in him. It's surely dehydrated by now. Earl, get me one of the feedbags and fill it half full of water. Also, give me one of the knapsacks the blankets are rolled in."

"Do you want the blankets, too?" I said.

"No, just the sack."

After four or five frightened swings of his head, the mustang realized the water was in the feedbag and slurped like crazy. Grandpa said we needed to sit awhile and let the horse regain his strength.

By mid-morning, the sun climbed high enough to stretch its warmth into the canyon, and the fog from our breaths disappeared.

Dad sat in quiet reflection while Grandpa told me more stories of the difficulties of digging the canal. The work was done from November to April because the growing season required the men and boys to tend to the crops at home to earn enough cash for the year and put up food for winter.

"You know, Earl, it was back-breaking dangerous work, but I believe it was harder on the women who never stepped foot in the canyon."

"Really?" I said.

"I'm afraid so. The women were left alone at home to take care of the children and the farm chores when the men and boys left on Monday morning and didn't return until Saturday afternoon. Most of Sunday was spent attending morning and evening services and recuperating. And on Monday, it started again. The men left with a clean set of clothes and another weeks' worth of food.

"The enthusiasm was high for the first few years, but there were years when we were discouraged, and we did not have the needed money. Many people felt we had no choice but to give up the effort: but a loan from the church in Salt Lake City came in the nick of time. From start to finish, it took us eleven years.

"Wow, I'm ten. It took a year longer than I have been living."

Grandpa's gaze sized me up. "Your Dad wasn't much older than you when he worked on the canal. He and your Uncle Whitney earned enough work credits to buy a twenty-acre farm plot and your city lot to split between them."

Grandpa stood. "Okay, boys. Let's try again to get this animal out of the ditch." He groaned as he straightened. "Oh, this getting old is hard work."

The refreshed mustang spooked when Grandpa eased into the mud and neighed and flung his head at Grandpa. "I figured as much," Grandpa said. "Here, hand me the knapsack."

I kept an eye on the stressed horse and eased close to the canal to hand the bag to Grandpa. He took the bag from me and gently coached the mustang to calm down. Grandpa slipped the sack over its head. The trapped horse protested once and then settled down.

Grandpa extended his hand toward me. "Hand me the shovel." He dug away more mud in front of the horse to the canal's edge and shaved the shoulder of the canal's wall to a slope.

Dad told me to take hold of one of the lariats and step away from the mustang. He said the canal trail wasn't wide enough to use our horses to tow the mustang in the direction he faced, so Dad and I would have to do our best to tug the mustang free.

On Grandpa's count of three, Dad and I tugged the ropes, and Grandpa slapped the hind end of the mustang. The horse rocked and lunged until one of its front legs, and then the other pulled loose. Its hindquarters remained stuck.

Grandpa held up a hand. "Hold up." The mustang calmed down and settled back in the mud. Its hindquarters hadn't moved an inch. "Let's let this stud catch its breath and gain strength, again." We waited four or five minutes, and then Grandpa motioned us forward and said, "Tighten your ropes. You won't be able to pull the horse free—we need to encourage him to fight to escape."

On three, again, Grandpa popped the horse's fanny and shouted, "Get out of here!" On its third lunge, its hindquarters came free from the mud. His front hooves pounded the bank. The horse stumbled to its front knees.

"Hold up, hold up," Grandpa said, and rested his hands against the horse's neck. We are about there. Let me remove this sack so he can see. I don't want him breaking loose and charging over the ledge." Grandpa huffed and took a deep breath. He slipped the bag from the animal's head. The wild horse whipped its head side to side.

"Are you doing okay, Earl?" Grandpa said.

"I'm fine."

"You okay, George?"

"Sure."

"Okay, this should do it," Grandpa said. "Watch out; there's no telling what this creature will do once it's freed."

When ready, Grandpa gave the signal again, and we tugged on the ropes. The mustang lunged and bucked. He pounded his front hooves and inched forward.

"Here, get up, horse, get out of here," Grandpa hollered with each slap on its rump.

The ground vibrated with the thuds of the mustang's hooves. I tugged with all my might.

The horse surged forward, fell once to its front knees, and then sprung from the canal. The sudden slack in the rope sent me stumbling backward, off the trail's ledge, down the steep slope. I held tight to the rope. I slid downward grinding against the coarse dirt and rocks. Dust flew around me. The mustang darted and yanked me across the face of the slope. Hemp fibers burned my palms. I grunted for strength as I tumbled across rocks and dirt. Finally, I had no choice but to let go of the rope.

CHAPTER 12   SATURDAY AFTERNOON

I was motionless for a second, but then my weight shifted downward. Dad and Grandpa hollered to me, but I didn't understand what they said. Downhill I slid. My hands were useless to slow my descent. Like a rag doll, I skipped and bounced downward feet first on my back. Suddenly my boot heel snared a scrawny tree and drove my knee to my chest. My heart pounded in my ears.

I peeked downhill but couldn't see the steep canyon wall beneath me, but could see the river a hundred feet below.

"Hang on, son," Dad hollered. "Lie still. We'll get a rope to you and get you back up top."

I heard a rope thump on the hillside just above me. Our saddle ropes were each thirty feet long, and a single one couldn't reach me.

"Earl, you're going to be fine," Grandpa said. "We will have to tie on a second rope to reach you."

On the second attempt, the rope slapped the ground to my side. I whimpered as I stretched my arm as far as I could but was three inches short of the rope.

On the next attempt, the rope popped my ear and flopped across my chest. I was never so grateful to be popped on my ear.

"Earl, tie the rope to your belt," Grandpa said.

My hands locked around the rope and trembled. With one leg sprawled downhill and the other caught on the scrub tree, it was hard to shove the rope beneath my belt. My hands fumbled, and I finally forced the rope between my belt and trousers. I knotted the rope four times.

"Are you ready?" Dad said.

I grasped the rope and scooted my fanny above the tree. "R- R- Ready." Nothing happened. "Ready!" I screamed.

The rope tightened and tugged my belt. The soil crunched beneath me, and loose rocks and sand tumbled below me. On the first tug, I was able to straighten my pinned leg. I rolled to my stomach. The dirt and rocks rustled beneath me with each tug from above. I spat dirt. Repeated tugs on the rope funneled dirt into my trousers.

Soon I was back on the canal trail. Dad helped me to my feet. "Are you all right, Son? Here, let me brush you off." Dad paused and suddenly wrapped his arms around me and wept. We both cried. After a moment, Dad said, "You didn't break anything, did you?"

My chest shuddered with a broken chuckle. "No, I'm fine, just scratched up."

"Thank goodness the little tree stopped you," Grandpa said.

I peeked over the edge and saw the path I'd carved in the loose soil. "I don't ever want to do that again," I said. "Did the mustang run away?"

"He ran like the wind," Dad said, "but thank goodness he collapsed before he ran away or we wouldn't have had the second rope to reach you."

"Oh yeah, I forgot the other two ropes were around his neck," I said.

"He staggered as he dragged you across the face of the hill. When you let go of the rope, he stumbled and fell on his side," Dad said.

Grandpa tilted his head and sighed. "Whew. Thank goodness he did. He floundered there for a while and gave me enough time to remove the ropes before he got to his feet and ran away."

* * *

It took us a couple of hours to shovel out the canal. I wondered if we could return home before dark. Mama thought we would be back in plenty of time for supper. I rested as Dad reshaped the canal's outer wall. "Dad, it's well past noon, and we haven't made it to the dam yet. How will Mama know we are running late? Aren't you afraid she might worry about us?"

"She'll know," Dad said.

"How? We're way out here in the canyon, and there's no way to tell her."

"We're sending a telegram."

"Telegram?" I said. I knew better, but I looked overhead. "There're no poles or wires."

"You're standing in it," Dad said.

I looked at my feet and then both directions of the canal. "What do you mean?"

"By now, the folks in Hurricane have received our message that we are repairing the canal."

"They have?"

"I guarantee they have. When Grandpa diverted the water from the canal last night, the water stopped arriving in the valley, they know."

"Oh, you're right," I said and laughed. "I would have never thought of that."

Dad smiled. "When we divert the water back into the canal, the water will reach Hurricane long before us, and they'll know we've made our repairs and are on our way home."

* * *

Shortly after noon, we saddled for the last portion of the ride to the dam. Grandpa said we were thirty minutes away from what he called the "headwaters" at the dam on the Virgin River.

Fresh shoeless horse tracks covered the trail. The river bottom came closer and closer as we continued upward on the canal's trail.

The canyon narrowed considerably, and the dam appeared a couple of hundred yards ahead.

"Wow!" I said.

"This is my favorite part of the ride," Grandpa said. "The canyon is narrowest here, the best place to build the dam. I love singing here and being accompanied by my echo. Let's all sing." He broke into Dad's favorite song again. "Oh, Danny boy, the pipes the pipes are calling, from glen to glen and down the mountainside ."

Grandpa sounded great between the rock walls. I believe he wanted to lift Dad's spirit and get his mind off Jennie. But Dad didn't join in.

Grandpa completed the song and became quiet. On a broader section of the canal path, I saw a spot where there were blackened fire rings and dugouts in the canyon wall, indicating people had camped there many times.

"Hey Grandpa, was this a campsite for the canal workers?"

He turned to look to his side. "Yes, it was. It was the first campsite the canal workers made. It was the most difficult to reach all the campsites. He pointed up the canyon wall. Every tool, all the food and cooking utensils, bedding, and workers had to come down the far canyon wall.

"Chinatown camp, where we slept last night, was the best and most used. Chinatown Wash was the largest area within the canyon to set up the cook tent, blacksmith works, and sleeping quarters. After our second year of ditch-digging, Isom Construction Company was contracted to construct an access road up along the river to the dam site. With the new road, we hauled in our tools and supplies instead of lowering and raising them on the canyon wall."

"Where did the name Chinatown come from?" I said.

Grandpa removed his hat and scratched the top of his head. "Well, there are two different stories. There was a Chinaman who cooked at the Silver Reef mine that came and cooked for us. Or, some folks say the dugouts the men carved into the gully's wall to sleep in looked like San Francisco's Chinatown hillside. But if you ask me, I don't believe anyone knows."

The dam was seventy-five feet high and forty feet wide. Until now, I had only seen the dam from the canyon's rim, four hundred feet above. I had heard many stories of the battles my grandmother Isom's brothers, who owned Isom Construction Company, fought and finally dammed the river after all their hard work washed away twice.

Grandpa pointed to a large flat boulder where the canal and the spillway left the river. "We'll eat a quick lunch and tend to the horses before we turn the water into the canal and head for home."

The sun shone on the bottom of the canyon and warmed the boulders. After I had a thick slice of bread, I laid back with my eyes closed to rest. The sun on my face and the warm stone felt great.

"Don't fall asleep on us, Earl," Grandpa said.

"I won't. I'm just thinking."

"Thinking?" Grandpa said. "That sounds dangerous."

Dad said, "While Earl is thinking, I'll inspect the dam and headgate. If things look good, I'll turn the water back into the canal, and we'll head down the trail."

"Take your time and be careful," Grandpa said.

I heard Dad walk away. With my fingers interlaced and tucked behind my head, I held my eyes closed and said, "Grandpa?"

"Yes, Earl."

"If God loves us and does miracles, why did he let Jennie die?"

Grandpa was quiet for a couple of seconds. "I wish I could tell you I knew, Earl—but I can't. Losing Jennie hurt us all, and we'll never forget her. Maybe one thing we can learn from losing Jennie is to appreciate the good things in our lives, especially our families and friends. God will take good care of Jennie, and we'll see her again."

I sat up. "Everyone prayed for Jennie. And Mama and Dad have always been good and kind, worked so hard for the church and us—it's not fair."

My eyes watered, and my chest tightened as I watched Dad, weary-looking, below inspecting the dam.

"Grandpa?" I said

"Yes, Earl."

"Why did Mama say Jennie's death was especially hard for Uncle Charles?"

Grandpa looked hesitant. "When did she say that?"

"I heard her tell Dad when Uncle Charles left our house the day after Jennie died, and I could tell she hoped I hadn't heard that."

"Your Uncle Charles had two young sisters die within four months of their birth."

I felt uncomfortable. "I've never heard that. How did the girls die?"

"This happened before there was a Hurricane. The Petty family lived in the town of Virgin back then. The first little girl, Jemima, died with cholera. We believe caused by bad water. The Virgin River is always muddy, and the water goes bad if it sits stagnant too long to settle out the mud."

Grandpa closed his fist and pointed his thumb toward the canal. "The canal is a blessing to the people of Hurricane; it provides safe drinking water."

"How did the second baby die?"

"I'm sure that's what is so difficult for Uncle Charles. She burned to death in the fireplace," Grandpa said.

I flinched. "Gosh, what happened?"

"At the time Charles was four years old, his dad, your Grandpa Petty, was often away from home for several days at a time hauling lumber to the Silver Reed mine or over to Lund's train station from the Petty family sawmill on Turnbull Mountain. Your Grandma Sarah Petty was left alone to raise the children and work the farm. It was late October and an unusually cold day. Your Grandma, Sarah, built a big fire in the fireplace to warm up the house. She laced a ribbon around baby Lucinda and tied her to a rocking chair placed in front of the fireplace and told little Charles to watch after her." Grandpa tilted his head. "And somehow the baby fell from the chair and into the fire. "

"Ooo..." The picture I saw in my head made me want to throw up.

"Charles, being such a little fellow, panicked and ran for his mother instead of trying to pull the baby from of the fire. The fire burned the baby severely by the time your grandmother got to her. The poor little girl suffered and died that night."

Grandpa removed his hat and raked his weathered fingers through his gray hair. He gazed at me and said, "Grandma blamed herself, but Charles has always felt guilty for not helping the baby instead of running to his mother."

"So you think Jennie made Uncle Charles remember his little sister?" I said.

Grandpa said. "I believe so."

Water gurgled in the canal.

Grandpa turned from me. "I see your Dad has turned the water back into the canal. It's time to head home." Grandpa pushed up from the boulder using both hands and took his first few steps bent and bow-legged. On his fourth or fifth steps, he straightened.

Dad trotted Dixie up alongside me as we saddled up. He gestured for me to take the trail lead with Lady.

"You want me to go first?"

He smiled and nodded.

Lady stepped to the front. I looked and saw Grandpa bringing up the rear.

Grandpa smiled big and said, "Earl, don't get us lost."

"I won't," I said, and then I remembered we were on the only canyon trail.

As we started down the trail, I could see where canal masons had cobbled stone wall shelves up from the canyon walls to carry the canal. I stopped Lady and glanced at Dad and Grandpa. "Wow, how did they do that?"

"It wasn't easy," Grandpa said. "We tried dynamiting a shelf in the canyon wall, but the rock formation was so loose the canyon wall would break up and slide to the canyon floor. The master masons figured out how to make it work. It was amazing to watch each day as it came together. The masons dug up, fired, and crushed limestone and made their masonry cement and chiseled the stones on site. "

"I wasn't able to see the stone walls were carrying the canal on our way up. It must be safe."

Grandpa laughed. "It's been there for twenty-five years."

"With all the dynamiting, was anyone ever hurt or killed?" I said.

Dad nodded slowly. "Yes. John Isom, a sixteen-year-old boy. He would have been Willie Isom's uncle. They were blasting up above on the canyon wall to clear loose rocks. When he thought everything had fallen and cleared, he peeked uphill from behind the ledge he had taken cover under, and at that moment, a straggling stone struck him in the forehead. The poor young man died instantly."

"Was he the only worker to die?" I said.

"No, a couple of years later, there was a seventeen-year-old drifter who worked with us for a few days. He complained of a bad headache and was told to go back to camp and see if the cook had something for him to take. He wasn't at camp when we knocked off in the afternoon. We searched both sides of the river for him, but all we found was what we thought were his footprints. It had rained heavily two days before, and the river was raging."

"Do you think he drowned in the river?"

"We don't know what happened. Several fellows searched the next couple days, but never found his body. It's sad to think of the boy dying so young and no way to notify his family."

* * *

The downhill return trip was more leisurely for the horses, and we made much better time. Neither the mountain lion nor the mustangs reappeared. I was just fine with not crossing the mountain lion's path again.

Exiting the canyon, I halted Lady and gazed to where we had been. Dad and Grandpa pulled up beside me. The canal and the trail cut a straight path along the canyon wall, but the river cascaded, flattened, and cascaded again. I realized the channel started near river level, rose as high as three hundred feet above the river at points, yet the river rose and met the channel at the dam, four hundred feet below the canyon rim.

I looked at Dad. "I got it," I said. "A straight line is the shortest distance between two points. The canal's slope is a straight line across the canyon wall, but the river falls, flattens, and falls many times."

Dad nodded his approval. "You got it."

I sat up straight, proud of myself.

* * *

We rode south along the base of Hurricane Hill. The sky was clear and bright. I looked across Hurricane Valley with a new appreciation for how beautiful the trees, the orchards, and the pastures were.

The last few miles were a breeze. Dad and Grandpa checked and rechecked each gate, which released water from the canal and sent it westward to homes and farm plots.

With our work done, we eased down a slight grade and loped across Highway 9. Grandpa trotted up alongside me.

"You tell your school mates the Hurricane Canal Company has added Earl Spendlove to its list of available ditch riders." He chuckled. "Earl and George, I'll see you at church tomorrow morning." Grandpa winked and peeled off from us and trotted up 300 Street toward his house.

"Goodbye, Grandpa, thank you," I yelled.

Dad rode up beside me. "Son, I need to tell you how proud I am of you for riding with Grandpa and me. Very few boys your age can ride the ditch." He stared into my eyes and nodded.

I felt good inside. I knew Dad loved me as much as he loved Jennie.

Dad leaned toward me and said in an even tone, "By the way, son, we don't need to tell your mama about your little slide down the hillside—not anytime soon."

Thoughts of my fall scared me again. "Yes, sir," I said. "But, but will you let me ride the ditch again?"

"You bet you. Good help is hard to find."

At East 200 North Street, we turned for home. I was tired but made myself sit up straight in my saddle and flare my elbows. Knowing she was nearing home, Lady pranced.

A block from home, I saw Tip on the front porch spring to his feet and yelp. He leaped clear of the three porch steps to the ground and raced toward us. His commotion brought Ruth to the front door. She stepped into the house and reappeared with Shirley and Mama behind her.

I tightened the reins on Lady. She had a bad habit of sprinting to the barn when our house came in sight.

"Welcome home," Mama said. "I'm glad to see you both return home in one piece." Her smile and her bright eyes had returned.

"How was the ride, Earl?"

"It was great! We saw four wild mustangs—and one of them got stuck in the canal, and we had to dig and pull him out."

Mama looked pleased. "You did? How did you do that?"

"It wasn't easy. Grandpa dug away the mud and Dad, and I tugged on the ropes tied around the horse's neck and when . . ."

Dad interrupted me. "We had the dickens of a time, but we managed to set the animal free—a beautiful large bay."

"Wow. Earl is so lucky," Shirley whined. "He got to see wild mustangs. I wish we could see them. He gets to do everything."

I crouched forward in my saddle. "It was neat, and we saw a big mean mountain lion, too!"

The joy in Mama's face disappeared. "A big mountain lion? How close did it get?" she said.

"It was uphill above Dad . . ."

"I never saw it before it went away," Dad said, and added, "Earl gathered enough rocks to fill both pants pockets and asked me to hold a few as well."

I figured he was changing the subject.

Mama laughed. "I am sure he did! I worried about you, boys," Mama said. "I'm glad you're home, safe, and sound. Earl, I know you learned a lot from your Dad and Grandpa. "

"Yes, Mama, I sure did."

Thinking I would show off a little at Shirley's expense, and I said. "Shirley, you probably don't know this, but it took a lot of arithmetic to build the canal." I held my two index fingers apart in front of me. "Sometimes the canal is three or four hundred feet below the top of the canyon," I motioned up and down, "and sometimes the canal is three or four hundred feet above the river, but somehow the canal starts just above the river and ends up at the river dam where the canal starts. So they had to figure out how to get from point A, at the low end of the canal, to point B, at the highest point of the canal." I looked to see if Mama was impressed.

Shirley thought for a moment. Ruth looked puzzled.

Shirley held out her index figure and drew in the air from my left index finger to my right index finger. "That's easy—a straight line."

Dad chuckled.

"Very good, Shirley," Mama said. "Why did you ask her that, Earl?"

"Oh, oh, never mind."

Mama said. "Come on, my boys; I'll have supper on the table by the time you wash up and put on a fresh change of clothes. We have to get you scrubbed well enough to return to church services in the morning. It will be so good to be with our dear friends again."

Dad spoke low. "I don't believe I would get anything from it."

Mama paused. "Well, please put away the horses and get cleaned up. Dr. Aiken is coming by after supper to check on us one last time."

CHAPTER 13   AFTER QUARANTINE

The next morning Willie Isom was right on-time and walked with us to Sunday school. He asked me a million questions about riding the canal as we led everyone to church—Mama held LaDean bundled on her shoulder, and Shirley and Ruth followed not far behind. When Ruth asked Mama where Dad was and if he was going to be late for Church, Mama bit her lower lip and shook her head and said, "He's not feeling well; he wanted us to go to church without him. He left the house early this morning."

At church, Grandpa Spendlove bragged on me to everyone. He said I surely was one of the best and youngest ditch riders, ever!

* * *

Dr. Aikens said no one contracted what Jennie had, so the quarantine hadn't been necessary—though it did give the family time together to grieve. Returning to school on Monday helped me feel as though things would get better. I guess to keep her mind off of Jennie, Mama kept busier than before, if that was possible. Dad said little, left home early each morning to work in the field, and returned home later than usual in the evening.

On Wednesday, Cousin Willie walked home with me after

school so I could ask Mama if I could go to his house to play. She said I could and asked me to carry a couple of slices of buttered bread to Dad since the Isom's home was in the direction of our farm plot. She quickly sliced and buttered the bread and wrapped the pieces in a cotton handkerchief made from an old tablecloth.

Careful not to mash Dad's treat, I trotted, and horse played with Willie across Main Street and the next few city blocks. As we approached our property, I told Willie to settle down while I called Dad.

Dad had his back to us. He was bent and steadily chopping the soil, but then he whacked the hoe forcefully into the ground and shouted something. I thought maybe Dad didn't want to be bothered, but then he stood, with his face to the sky, and shouted angrily. He hadn't heard me. Dad spoke his mind to God, bitter and hurt. He then shuddered and cried.

My throat and chest tightened. It was the same feeling I had when I saw Dad cry the night Jennie died. My eyes swelled with tears.

"What's wrong with your Dad?" Willie said.

At first, I couldn't say anything. "Hush, Willie. There's nothing wrong with him."

"Who is he talking to? Boy, he's mad!"

"Nobody," I said. I wished I hadn't come, especially with Willie. I stared at the handkerchief. "I don't think he wants this. Let's go before he sees us. And please don't tell your Mama and Dad what we saw."

Playing at Willie's wasn't fun. I kept seeing and hearing Dad in the field alone and crying. I cried as I walked home, and I feared I might run into Dad on his way home. When I came through the back door, Mama was in front of the stove preparing supper. Without looking at me, she said. "Did you have fun?"

"Um, yes, ma'am."

"How was your Dad? Was he pleased with his surprise?"

I froze at the top of the basement stairs. "I . . . I forgot to take it to him and I left it at Willie's." The last thing I wanted to do was tell Mama a lie, but I couldn't tell her what I saw.

"Earl . . ." she said. "You disappoint me. Your dad would have enjoyed that. Go wash up for supper."

Dad came home as we were sitting down at the kitchen table. He said he would eat something later and went to his room.

* * *

Instead of getting better, Dad seemed to get worst. Both Mama and Dad often cried together, but Mama showed even more love for us children, and Dad got quieter and quieter. I came home from school Friday and found Mama staring out the kitchen window.

"I'm home, Mama," I said as I placed my Reader on the kitchen table and reached for the back door.

"You need to stay in the house," Mama said. "Grandpa Spendlove and your Dad are having a talk, so don't bother them."

"Yes, ma'am, can I have something to eat?"

"You sure can. I made some cookies this morning. Where are Shirley and Ruth?" Mama removed a plate of sugar cookies from the cupboards.

"They're across the street at the Stouts playing with Alta and Rae," I said.

Mama smiled and shook her head. "Poor Mary Stout, fifteen children of her own and the neighborhood children, want to play at her house—and she's fine with it. If there ever were two saints here on earth, it would be Marion and Mary Stout."

LaDean whimpered in Mama and Dad's room as she woke from her afternoon nap. Mama scurried to comfort her. "Why, hello, Sweetie. Did you sleep well?" I heard Mama say.

I stepped to the window and saw Grandpa Spendlove and Dad with their backs to the house and their elbows resting on the corral's top fence rail. They stood there for the longest time, not saying a word and gazing straight ahead.

Finally, Grandpa said a few words, patted Dad on his back, mounted Casper, and rode out the rear gate.

Dad ate supper with us that night. He ate very little, but he did ask each of us kids how our day was.

Dad was already dressed for church when Mama woke me the next Sunday morning. But at church, it wasn't the same as before. It was the first time I saw Dad at church without his well-worn leather-bound scriptures. He smiled and spoke softly when other members welcomed him and expressed their sympathy. Their faces showed they understood. Mama's eyes stayed wet, and her smile was tight-lipped.

The next Sunday, Dad left home before we dressed for church. Mama said Dad wasn't comfortable going to church and told us, kids, to hurry and get ready.

* * *

One afternoon on my way to rake out the stalls, Dad was in our side yard pruning fruit trees, and I heard him cursing and asking God "why." My stomach soured, and I ran as fast as I could to the barn. I never told anyone.

Mama was the strong one for the family. She would sob sometimes, but she steered us kids and maintained the household. We hadn't had a family prayer since Jennie died, and as a special favor to Mama, Dad agreed, and we resumed Morning Prayer before our busy days.

One evening, Mama asked me to walk to our farm plot and tell Dad supper was ready. I dreaded the moment. With the shorter autumn days, the sunlight had nearly faded from Hurricane. I could see my breath in the late November air as I made my way across the empty streets. At the edge of our eleven acres, I searched for Dad's darkened figure working the rows of sugar beets. Fear chilled me when I couldn't find him, but before I called for him, I heard the ping of a hoe blade in the rocky desert soil at the far front corner. Dad was bent and hoeing steadily.

And then, in his mellow tones, I heard Dad begin singing, "Oh Danny Boy, the pipes, the pipes are calling . . ." His voice carried well in the thin desert air, and as he sang, his voice became louder.

My lungs swelled with the cold evening air. The weight I carried around on my chest lifted. "Dad?" I said.

He paused and looked at me. "Hello, Earl. I didn't see you there."

"Mama said supper would be ready soon."

Dad swung the hoe up and rested it on his shoulder. "Good, I'm hungry."

* * *

I knew Dad would always hurt to hold Jennie, and the family would forever long to have her with us and wonder what she would have been like as she grew up. But finally hearing Dad sing again, I knew we were past the worst. Losing Jennie was unfair but we could choose to be happy still as a family - even with Shirley.

THE END

EPILOGUE

George and Lilly's youngest daughter, Dorothy Spendlove, lived in the family house until it was sold in the early 1960s.

When the house was cleared of furnishings, a small wooden box was found in the parents' closet. Inside was found Jennie's scuffed brown shoes, the tin can that kept Jennie's medicine coins and the lock of her hair tied with a pink ribbon.

Please provide your Amazon review of DITCH RIDER

Steven R. Stewart is the author of *DITCH RIDER*, a historical fiction based on his dear late uncle, Earl Spendlove, as a ten-year-old boy in 1923 in the desert of southern Utah. He has also written, *UNTO THE LEAST OF THESE*, a historical fiction which portrays the seldom-told story about the anti-secession sentiments in the upstate of South Carolina, during the American Civil War. Actual events and historical characters brought to light through the tenacious fictional character, emancipated Will 'Homey" Jones, in his struggle to claim his entitled God-given respect and dignity. *UNTO THE LEAST OF THESE* will be published in late December 2019, on Amazon Paperback and Kindle KDP.

Steve credits his writing development (a true work-in-progress) to several Greenville Technical College creative writing courses, the excellent critiques, and guidance from fellow members of the Greenville Chapter of the South Carolina Writers Association, and encouragement from his large extended family.

A Georgia native and Auburn University graduate, Steve resides in beautiful upstate South Carolina with his wife, Ann. Two of his adult sons live in Huntsville, Alabama, while the other two sons live in Greenville, South Carolina.

Contact Steve at *sstewsc@aol.com*

Please provide your book review on Amazon Paperback, Kindle KDP, or Kindle Select.

BIBLIOGRAPHY

I Was Called to Dixie, Andrew Karl Larson, Deseret News Press, Salt Lake City, Utah
> First edition, 1961
> Second printing, 1979
> Third printing, 1992

Portraits of the Hurricane Pioneers by Janice Force DeMille, Homestead Publishers, Dixie College Press, 1976

Unpublished family histories in my possession with one or more narratives by:
Earl Petty Spendlove
Shirley Spendlove Glore
Ruth Spendlove Memmott
LaDean Spendlove Stewart
Clark Spendlove
Dorothy Spendlove

Made in the USA
Coppell, TX
10 May 2021